WORTH THE RISK

AN ENEMIES TO LOVERS ROMANCE

WORTH IT ALL
BOOK 1

LIZ DURANO

**Some partnerships are worth the risk.
Others are designed to break your heart.**

Highland Community Center isn't just a building—it's my
father's legacy, my neighborhood's heart, and the only home
my Filipino-American community has ever known. So when
Pierce Enterprises announces plans to demolish Highland
for luxury condos, I'm ready to fight.

What I'm not ready for is Declan Pierce himself.

The devastatingly handsome CEO should be easy to hate.
Instead, I find myself glimpsing something unexpected
beneath his corporate armor—vulnerability that calls to me
despite every logical reason to keep my guard up.

When he proposes an unlikely collaboration to find
preservation alternatives, I face an impossible choice.
Trust the enemy who could destroy everything I've fought to
protect, or miss our only chance for survival.

I've spent my life believing people can change. But what
happens when transformation might be the most dangerous
lie of all?

1

Maya

I'm not usually like this—barging into corporate lobbies like some kind of crusader. But eight hundred and forty-three signatures will do that to a person.

Sure, I'm passionate, but not the confrontational kind. Not the woman who storms marble-floored fortresses in sensible flats and a blazer that's seen better board meetings. Yet here I am, clutching this manila folder like it contains state secrets instead of petition signatures, my heart hammering against my ribs.

Eight hundred and forty-three neighbors who showed up when I knocked on their doors. Eight hundred and forty-three people who believe Highland Community Center is worth saving. Eight hundred and forty-three voices Pierce Enterprises has been ignoring for six months.

"Ma'am, do you have an appointment?" The receptionist's voice slices through my resolve.

I approach her imposing desk, shoulders back, chin up—the posture my father always said commanded respect. "I need to see Declan Pierce. It's about Highland Community Center."

Her manicured fingers never pause in their typing. "Mr. Pierce doesn't take unscheduled meetings. If you'd like to make an appointment—"

"I've been trying to make an appointment for six months." Every ignored email, every transferred call sits in those words. "Six months of runarounds while you people plan to destroy everything my father built."

Now she looks up, her expression shifting from bored professionalism to cautious alarm. "Ma'am, I'm going to need you to lower your voice—"

"My voice is perfectly reasonable." I lean forward, palms flat on the cold marble. "What's unreasonable is a corporation bulldozing a community center that's served downtown LA for twenty years without so much as a conversation."

Behind me, the elevator chimes. Expensive shoes whisper across marble. I don't turn—can't afford to lose this momentum, not when Jessica is finally reaching for her phone with obvious reluctance.

"Is there a problem here?"

The voice carries the kind of authority that makes spines straighten involuntarily. Deep, cultured, probably used to being obeyed.

Perfect. Someone with actual power.

I turn around, and—

Putang ina...

I'd done my research the moment we received that impersonal eviction letter. Declan Pierce, thirty-two, heir to a real estate empire, Harvard MBA, Olympic rower. Made his billions when a social media startup he'd backed in college exploded into one of the biggest platforms in the world. A man who moved fast and broke things, then donated enough to charity that people forgot about the casualties. I'd watched conference videos where he smirked like the world was full of chess pieces he could move at will.

But research doesn't capture presence.

Declan Pierce is devastating in the way expensive things are—perfectly crafted, elegantly designed, completely untouchable. The charcoal suit fits like it was cut specifically for his frame, and there's something about the way he holds himself that suggests he's never doubted his right to any space he occupies.

"Mr. Pierce." I force my voice steady, reminding myself why I'm here. "I'm Maya Navarro from Highland Community Center. I've been trying to reach you about the Anderson Project."

Something flickers across his expression—surprise, maybe recognition. Or who knows? Maybe indifference. I can barely think straight.

This is the man who wants to erase my father's legacy with a signature on a demolition order.

"Miss Navarro, I believe my development team has been in communication with your organization."

"Communication?" My voice climbs despite my best efforts. "You mean the form letter informing us Highland would be demolished for luxury condos? That communication?"

His jaw tightens almost imperceptibly. "Perhaps we should continue this conversation in my office."

"Perhaps we should." I clutch the folder like a shield. "I

have eight hundred and forty-three reasons why the Anderson Project should be reconsidered."

We stare at each other across the gleaming lobby. I feel Jessica's curious gaze, the subtle attention of other employees who've slowed their purposeful stride to witness this—David challenging Goliath on his home turf.

"Very well." He gestures toward the elevators. "Fifteen minutes."

"I'll take whatever time I need."

The corner of his mouth twitches. Annoyance or amusement—impossible to tell. "Fifteen minutes, Miss Navarro. That's more than most people get."

The elevator climbs to the thirtieth floor in suffocating silence. When the doors part, I follow him down a hallway lined with expensive art and floor-to-ceiling windows showcasing the city sprawling below. Highland is down there somewhere—a small rectangle of hope in the urban maze, its days numbered if I fail here.

Declan's office screams success in the most impersonal way possible. Massive. Spotless. Dominated by a desk that probably costs more than Highland's annual budget. Awards and certificates march across the walls like conquests—Pierce Enterprises reshaping Los Angeles one development at a time.

"Please, sit." He moves behind his desk without sitting himself, silhouetted against the afternoon sun.

"I prefer to stand." I open my folder, place the petition on his pristine surface. The letterhead catches the light—*Highland Community Center, Founded 2005, Alejandro Navarro.* My throat tightens seeing Papa's name there, his careful signature on the incorporation papers still visible through the folder's plastic sleeve.

"Highland Community Center has served the Filipino-American community for twenty years. We provide after-school programs for over two hundred children, job training for adults, cultural preservation classes—"

"I'm aware of Highland's... contributions." He glances at the papers without touching them.

"Contributions?" The word scrapes my throat. "Highland isn't just a building, Mr. Pierce. It's my father's dream made real. When he arrived from the Philippines with nothing but hope and twenty-seven dollars, he saw Filipino families struggling alone in a new country. So he rented a storefront, painted the walls himself, and created a place where we could belong."

I touch the petition, Papa's name still visible on the letterhead. "Highland is where teenagers learn traditional dances so they don't forget who they are. Where Lola Soledad brings her grandchildren when their parents work double shifts. When Papa died two years ago, the entire community gathered there to honor him—because Highland was his gift to all of us."

"It's a building on prime downtown real estate." His voice cuts through my passion with surgical precision. "Serving a very small demographic in a city that desperately needs housing."

My carefully planned arguments crumble. "Small demographic? We serve over three thousand people directly. Those people matter, Mr. Pierce. They have lives, families—"

"And they'll still have those things when Highland relocates."

"Relocates?" My voice cracks. "Where? You've made no provisions in any document we've seen. You're not moving Highland—you're erasing it."

For the first time, his composure wavers. He reaches for a file, sets it down unopened. "The Anderson Project will provide much-needed housing—"

"Luxury condos starting at eight hundred thousand dollars." I've done my homework. "That's not housing for people in this neighborhood. That's housing for people like you."

The words slice between us. His eyes narrow, and something dangerous flickers beneath the polish.

"People like me?" Soft voice, steel underneath.

Heat burns my cheeks, but I don't retreat. "The kind who sees dollar signs where others see home. Who thinks profit margins matter more than people."

"The kind who understands development creates jobs, generates tax revenue, contributes to economic growth." He steps closer—expensive cologne, coffee, the weight of a long day. "Who deals in reality instead of sentiment."

"Sentiment?" My folder tumbles from numb fingers, scattering petition sheets across his pristine carpet. Papa's incorporation papers flutter to the floor, his signature face-up like an accusation. "My father didn't just build Highland from nothing—he built it with his bare hands. Painted every wall, installed every light fixture, because he couldn't afford contractors. He poured twenty years of sixteen-hour days into that place."

I kneel, gathering the scattered legacy. "The night before

he died, Papa made me promise to protect Highland. Not just the building—his life's work. His proof that immigrants don't just take from this country, we give back." I stand, papers trembling in my grip. "That's not sentiment—that's sacred trust."

The hard edges of his face seem to soften for a heartbeat, but as quickly as it comes, it's gone. "Your fifteen minutes are up, Miss Navarro."

I collect the scattered papers, hands trembling with fury and something else—an unwelcome awareness of how his proximity affects my breathing, how his voice saying my name sends treacherous flutters through my chest.

I stand, clutching the rumpled petition, leaving the rest of the sheets by his feet like fallen soldiers. "This isn't over."

His storm-gray eyes lock on mine. "I don't imagine it is."

I walk toward the door, spine straight despite the tears threatening at the corners of my eyes. Months of planning, hoping, fighting—and I've failed to move him even an inch.

At the door, I turn back. He's still watching me with an unreadable expression.

"Six weeks." My voice doesn't shake. "That's all the time you've given us before demolition begins. Six weeks to find somewhere else for eight hundred and forty-three people to gather, celebrate, belong." I meet his stare. "My father spent twenty years building something beautiful. You'll destroy it in six weeks for luxury condos most of our families could never afford."

The papers on his floor catch the light—Papa's careful handwriting, his dream reduced to scattered documents. "I hope it's worth it, Mr. Pierce. I hope when you're cashing those checks, you remember the man who built what you're tearing down."

Inside the elevator, I allow myself thirty seconds to fall apart—thirty seconds for tears, for shaking hands, for the crushing weight of failing Papa's dying wish, the promise I made to protect his life's work, and I couldn't even get fifteen minutes to matter—then I wipe my eyes, straighten my shoulders, and start planning.

Highland Community Center survived twenty years in downtown LA. Economic downturns, natural disasters, the slow creep of gentrification. Papa built it to last, and I'll be damned if I let some privileged CEO tear down what took him a lifetime to create.

It will survive Declan Pierce, too.

Even if part of me can't stop thinking about the moment his composure cracked, or the way my name sounds in his voice, or the fact that for just an instant, I thought I saw something real beneath all that expensive armor.

Focus, Maya. Papa's legacy is what matters.

But as the elevator carries me back to ground level, I can't shake the feeling that this war just became a lot more complicated.

Declan

As SOON AS the elevator doors close behind Maya Navarro, the silence in my office feels deafening.

Her final words echo in the space she's vacated, each syllable cutting deeper than the rest. *My father spent twenty years building something beautiful. You'll destroy it in six weeks for luxury condos.*

Eight hundred and forty-three families. The number sits on my chest like a stone.

I move to the windows overlooking downtown Los Angeles, pressing my palm against the cool glass as Maya's accusations replay in my mind. Six months of silence. No transition assistance. No alternative programming locations. No support for families who've depended on Highland's services for decades.

That can't be right. Pierce Enterprises has protocols for community displacement—comprehensive transition programs I personally approved three years ago when I took over from my father. When we develop properties that house community services, we don't just shut them down without offering alternatives. We're not that kind of company.

Are we?

The thought sends ice through my veins. I've spent three years trying to modernize Pierce Enterprises, to move beyond my father's more ruthless approaches to development. Community engagement initiatives, transition support programs, stakeholder communication protocols—I implemented all of it to ensure we weren't the corporate bulldozer Maya clearly believes us to be.

But if Highland has been stonewalled for six months...

I press the intercom button. "Jessica, what transition support have we offered Highland Community Center since we informed them of the building's demolition?"

There's a pause—the kind that makes my chest tighten with dread. Jessica's voice crackles through, hesitant. "I'll need to check with Mr. Gordon's office. He took over that file about six months ago."

Harrison Gordon. My father's former right-hand man, current Chairman of Pierce Enterprises' board, the man who supposedly taught me everything about responsible development. The man who reports to me but somehow managed to control Highland's case for six months without my knowledge.

"Get me everything," I say, voice deceptively calm. "Every email, every letter, every phone log. And Jessica? Do it quietly."

"Of course, Mr. Pierce."

I end the call and return to the window, Los Angeles sprawling beneath me like a circuit board of ambition and broken promises. The afternoon light slants through the floor-to-ceiling windows, casting long shadows across the pristine hardwood. Everything in this office speaks of control, of power carefully wielded, yet somehow Harrison has been operating completely outside my oversight.

Maya's words circle my thoughts like vultures. *Six months of being shuffled around and given the runaround while you people plan to destroy everything my father built.* The fire in her dark eyes when she said it—deep brown with flecks of amber that caught the light—as they held mine without flinching. The way her voice cracked slightly when she spoke about her father's dying wish, the promise she made to protect his legacy.

She's beautiful, but not in the polished, predictable way of the society women who typically orbit my world. Maya Navarro has substance. Depth. The kind of passionate conviction that radiates from every gesture, every word, every defiant tilt of her chin when she faced me down in my own office.

When she spoke about Highland Community Center, about the families depending on its services, her entire being seemed to vibrate with purpose. Twenty-seven dollars and a dream that became a community center serving three thousand people. My father came to Los Angeles with considerably more capital, but the drive was the same— build something, leave a mark, create a legacy that would outlast the man who built it.

Highland's entire annual operating budget is roughly $180,000 according to the financial documents my team compiled months ago. Less than what I spend on wine in a year, yet they've built something that's lasted twenty years and serves thousands of people.

But if Harrison has been systematically ignoring their requests for basic communication...

My inbox fills with six months of correspondence—or rather, Highland's increasingly desperate attempts at correspondence. Email after email from Maya and other board members, each one more carefully worded than the last. Professional inquiries about relocation assistance. Requests for meetings to discuss transition timelines. Proposals for temporary space during construction. Offers to work with Pierce Enterprises on community impact mitigation.

None of them answered. Not a single reply in six months.

I scroll through Maya's messages, watching her tone evolve from hopeful to frustrated to grimly determined. Her early emails are almost apologetic, as if she's afraid of taking up too much corporate time. *I understand how busy your schedule must be, but when you have a moment, we'd love to discuss Highland's future...* Professional. Respectful. Patient.

By month two, there's steel beneath the politeness. *We've submitted three formal requests for meetings and haven't received acknowledgment. As Highland serves over 3,000 community members, we need to begin planning for service continuity...*

By month three, she's citing legal precedents and community impact studies. *Los Angeles Municipal Code requires 90-day notice for displacement of community services. We received 60 days for lease termination with no discussion of transition assistance...*

By month four, her emails become more frequent, more urgent. *Children's after-school programs end in eight weeks with no alternative location identified. Families are asking questions we can't answer because Pierce Enterprises won't respond to our communications...*

Month five brings barely controlled desperation. *We've attempted contact through every available channel. Twenty-seven phone calls to your office have been transferred or gone unreturned. This is not acceptable business practice...*

By month six, she'd stopped emailing altogether. Instead, she was in my lobby with a folder full of signatures and a heart full of righteous fury, given fifteen minutes to plead her case to the CEO who'd been oblivious to her community's plight.

The intercom crackles. "Mr. Pierce? Mr. Gordon is here to see you."

Perfect timing. "Send him in."

Harrison enters with the practiced ease of someone who's shaped this company longer than I've been alive. At sixty-two, he's everything I used to think I'd become—silver-haired, expensively dressed, utterly unmoved by what he'd dismiss as "sob stories about community centers and immigrant dreams." He settles into the leather chair across from my desk as if he owns it.

"Declan, I understand you had an interesting visitor this afternoon." His tone carries the casual authority of a man who's been Maxwell Pierce's voice for decades, even two years after my father's death.

"Maya Navarro. She's concerned about Highland Community Center's transition process."

Harrison's laugh is sharp, humorless. "Transition process? That's a generous way to describe it. The woman stormed our lobby demanding meetings she has no right to expect."

Something cold settles in my stomach. "What compensation has Highland received for their displacement?"

"Standard notice. Sixty days, as required by law." He adjusts his tie with casual indifference. "They've had six months to figure out their situation since we terminated their lease."

"And assistance? Moving costs? Program transition support? Alternative space recommendations?"

His smile doesn't reach his eyes. "What are we, a charity? Those aren't legal requirements, Declan, and you know it."

The pieces click with sickening clarity. "Harrison, what happened to our community displacement protocols? The transition programs I approved when I took over?"

"Suggestions, not requirements." He waves a dismissive hand. "I prefer efficiency over hand-holding."

Heat rises in my chest. "Hand-holding? We're talking about a community center that serves three thousand people. Highland has been operating for twenty years—this isn't hand-holding, it's basic corporate responsibility."

"Corporate responsibility is to our shareholders, not every neighborhood organization that thinks they're entitled to special treatment." Harrison's voice sharpens with the authority of a man who's been having this argument longer than I've been in business. "We provide legal notice, they find alternative arrangements. Simple."

I stand, pacing to the windows. "Why wasn't I involved in Highland's case from the beginning?"

"Because I've been handling community relations since your father founded this company thirty-five years ago." The paternal tone creeps in—the same voice that used to comfort me after Maxwell's more brutal business lessons, now wielded like a weapon. "And because I know better than to let personal feelings interfere with business decisions."

"Personal feelings?" I turn back to face him. "This is about our reputation. About not creating exactly the kind of community opposition we're dealing with now. Maya Navarro organized eight hundred and forty-three signatures in six months because we gave her no other choice."

"Opposition we can manage with legal teams and security contractors." Harrison stands, straightening his suit with practiced authority. "What we don't do is blur the lines between corporate strategy and community charity work."

"Since when is basic communication charity work?"

"Since it encourages dependency and entitlement." His eyes narrow. "Declan, your father never would have questioned these methods. Maxwell understood that business success requires difficult decisions, not community hand-holding."

There it is. My father's ghost, summoned to end the argument. Maxwell Pierce—the man who built an empire through ruthless efficiency and calculated distance from the communities his developments displaced. The man whose shadow still shapes every board meeting, every strategic decision, every moment Harrison thinks I'm being too soft for the family business.

"My father also didn't have to deal with social media and community organizing," I say carefully. "Times change, Harrison. Our approaches should change with them."

"Some principles don't change." Harrison moves toward the door, then pauses. "Like the difference between running a business and running a charity. Like understanding that every dollar we spend on community relations is a dollar that doesn't go to shareholders or company growth."

I think about Maya's folder of signatures, her father's incorporation papers scattered on my office floor. "What if treating Highland as a charity case creates more expensive problems than treating them as stakeholders?"

Harrison's expression hardens. "Then we handle problems as they arise. We don't prevent them by encouraging every community group to think they deserve corporate welfare."

"Community welfare?" My voice rises despite my efforts to stay controlled. "Harrison, Highland serves three thousand people. Their annual budget is less than my entertainment expenses. We're not talking about welfare—we're talking about basic human decency."

"Human decency doesn't pay dividends." Harrison's tone grows colder. "And it certainly doesn't justify the precedent you'd set by giving special treatment to every organization that comes crying to our offices."

"Maya Navarro wasn't crying. She was fighting for her community."

"Same difference. Both emotional responses that have no place in business strategy." Harrison adjusts his tie again. "Declan, I need to know that you understand the distinction between effective leadership and sentimental decision-making. Your father never would have made that mistake."

The words hit like a physical blow. Harrison knows exactly which buttons to push—my father's memory, my leadership credibility, the fear that I'm not ruthless enough to run Pierce Enterprises successfully.

"Maybe Maxwell was wrong about some things."

The silence that follows is deafening. Harrison's expression shifts from paternal authority to something approaching alarm.

"Be very careful, son." His voice drops to barely above a whisper. "Your father built this company on principles that work. Principles that created the wealth and influence you inherited. I won't watch you destroy his legacy because some community activist got under your skin."

Some community activist. As if Maya Navarro is just another obstacle to be cleared rather than someone fighting to honor her dead father's dream.

"This conversation isn't over," I say.

"Yes, it is." Harrison straightens his suit jacket with finality. "I've been protecting this company—and you—from exactly these kinds of emotional decisions since Maxwell died. Don't make me question whether you're ready to lead Pierce Enterprises, or whether the board needs to reconsider your authority over community relations decisions."

The threat hangs in the air like smoke. Harrison controls the board through decades of relationships and Maxwell's enduring influence. Harrison speaks with my father's authority, wields my father's methods, and can make my leadership very difficult if I don't fall in line with the Pierce Enterprises way of doing business.

After he leaves, silence settles around me like a burial shroud, the weight of the conversation settling on my shoulders. Three years of trying to modernize this company, and Harrison has been systematically undermining my efforts with cases like Highland.

How many other community organizations have been stonewalled? How many other Maya Navarros have given up fighting because Pierce Enterprises made engagement impossible?

I pull up Highland's file on my computer, hoping for more documentation. Two documents in an otherwise empty folder—a lease non-renewal notice dated six months ago, and the legal demolition notice sent this week. No follow-up communication between Pierce and Highland. No assistance offers. No acknowledgment that Highland serves families who've depended on their programs for decades.

Just as Harrison described—legal obligations met, human obligations ignored completely.

My phone buzzes with a text from Elliot Walker, my best friend and VP of development:

> Heard you met the infamous Maya Navarro.
> How'd that go?

I stare at the message, thinking about Maya's amber-flecked eyes and Harrison's systematic stonewalling. About the way her voice cracked when she talked about her father's twenty-seven dollars and twenty-year dream. About the incorporation papers scattered on my floor like fallen soldiers in a war she didn't even know she was fighting.

DECLAN:

> Complicated. But educational.

ELLIOT:

> Good complicated or bad complicated?

DECLAN:

> The kind that makes me question how
> we've been handling community relations.

ELLIOT:

Uh oh. That sounds like the beginning of a
very expensive educational process.

DECLAN:

Maybe. But maybe some things are worth
the investment.

I set down my phone and lean back in my chair. Harrison thinks he's protecting the company—and my father's legacy —by treating communities like obstacles to be cleared rather than stakeholders to be managed. But Maya just proved that approach creates exactly the kind of opposition that threatens business success.

More than that, it makes us the villains in our own story. The corporate bulldozer she accused us of being.

The intercom buzzes. "Mr. Pierce? Your two-thirty with the Westside Development team is here."

"Give me ten minutes."

I close Maya's emails, but her words linger like accusations in the air. The way she said "you people" with such controlled fury. The tremor in her voice when she mentioned families depending on Highland's after-school programs. The way she clutched those petition signatures like armor against corporate indifference.

The Anderson Project represents a forty-million-dollar investment opportunity. I can't let one community advocate derail the entire development. But maybe I can change how we approach it.

Harrison wants to manage opposition with legal teams and security contractors—my father's old playbook for dealing with community resistance. But what if we managed resistance with partnership instead of intimidation? What if we gave Maya Navarro exactly what she's been asking for six months—a seat at the table, a voice in Highland's future, a real chance to save what her father built?

Not charity. Strategy.

Highland serves three thousand people in the heart of downtown LA. Those three thousand people have friends, families, social networks that extend throughout the city. They vote in local elections, participate in community organizations, influence neighborhood dynamics that can make or break development projects.

Maya organized eight hundred and forty-three signatures in six months while being systematically ignored. Imagine what she could accomplish with actual support, with Pierce Enterprises as a partner rather than an adversary.

Harrison won't like it. The board might question it. My father's ghost will certainly disapprove. But as I straighten my tie and prepare for my next meeting, one thing becomes crystal clear: I'd rather deal with their disapproval than become the kind of man Maya thinks I am.

The kind of man my father apparently was.

3

———

Maya

"Ate Maya, where do you want the sound system?"

I look behind me to see Carlo Martinez wheeling in a portable speaker, his fifteen-year-old frame dwarfed by the equipment. His mother, Rosa, follows behind him with a thermos of coffee and the kind of determined expression that built Highland Community Center one volunteer at a time.

"By the front entrance," I tell him, checking my phone for the tenth time as I stand in Highland's main hall surrounded by poster board and enough coffee to fuel a small revolution.

Six AM. In two hours, we'll march from Highland to Pierce Enterprises, and I have no idea if anyone will show up besides the usual suspects—the core group of families who've been with us through everything.

"Anak, here. I made siopao. This one is bola bola. With egg." Rosa presses a white steamed bun into my hands, still warm from her kitchen. "You can't lead a protest on an empty stomach."

This is why Highland matters—not just because it's a building, but because it's filled with people like Rosa who show up at dawn with homemade breakfast and volunteer their teenage sons to haul sound equipment. People who call me *anak* like I'm their own daughter.

"Thank you." I take a bite, though my stomach is too knotted with nerves to properly appreciate Rosa's cooking. The familiar flavors of garlic and ginger should be comforting, but all I can think about is how many people might actually show up, and whether any of this will matter to a man who can ignore eight hundred and forty-three signatures.

"Has anyone heard from the Times reporter?" I call out.

"I'm handling media," comes the crisp response from across the room. Lianne Peralta emerges from behind a stack of protest signs, phone pressed to her ear and that familiar look of controlled efficiency that makes her so successful at running Luminous Events. Even at six AM, coordinating a community protest between client calls, she looks like she stepped out of a business magazine.

Lianne ends her call and gives me a thumbs-up. "Confirmed—the Times, Channel 7, and KPCC. Plus, someone from the Downtown News said they'd try to make it." She consults her phone with the same precision she uses to coordinate celebrity galas. "We've got sixty-seven confirmed on Facebook, but you know how social media goes."

I do know. Digital activism doesn't always translate to bodies on the street. But as I watch Lianne seamlessly juggle Highland's protest logistics with what sounds like a high-profile wedding planning call, I'm reminded why we've been best friends since college. Where I'm all intensity and righteous anger, Lianne is pure strategic charm.

Of course, we've been planning this protest for weeks. My visit to Pierce Enterprises yesterday was spontaneous frustration, but organizing a hundred people takes time.

"Maya?" A familiar voice makes me turn. Enrique de Leon stands in the doorway, and the expression on his weathered face tells me everything I need to know about why he's here so early.

Tito Ricky—my father's closest friend and Highland's volunteer legal counsel—has been my surrogate father since Papa died. Which means he's about to give me advice I probably don't want to hear.

"Can we talk?" He gestures toward the office.

I follow him past the photos lining Highland's walls—twenty years of community events, graduations, cultural celebrations. Papa's smiling face appears in dozens of them, and I catch my reflection in the glass covering his portrait. Same determined jaw, same fire in our dark eyes. Same stubborn refusal to back down from a fight.

Tito Ricky closes the office door and settles into the chair across from Papa's old desk—my desk now, though I still think of it as his.

"I've been researching Pierce Enterprises," he says without preamble. "Their development pattern shows they've demolished twelve community facilities in the past five years. Three of those under Declan Pierce personally."

I stare at Tito Ricky. Three communities destroyed since Declan took over. So much for thinking he might be different from his father.

"Churches, community centers, affordable housing—all replaced with luxury developments," Tito Ricky continues. "Their strategy focuses on transit-oriented development, maximizing property values near Metro stations."

"What's your point, Tito?"

"My point is that Declan Pierce is exactly who you think he is. Which means polite presentations won't work. We need to prepare for a real fight."

Before I can respond, the office door bursts open. Lianne appears, breathless and clutching her phone.

"Maya, you need to see this." She shoves the screen toward me—Pierce Enterprises' stock price from yesterday's close, down three points.

"I don't understand what this has to do with us."

"The Metro expansion hit major delays," Lianne explains, her event planner instincts for timing and logistics in full display. "Underground utility conflicts. Since downtown developments bank on that transit hub, investors are spooked about the whole corridor."

I stare at the numbers. "If Pierce focuses on transit-oriented development..."

"Then they have bigger problems than Highland," Tito Ricky says, leaning back with the first smile I've seen from him all morning. "Sometimes the best strategy is letting your opponent fight battles on multiple fronts."

My phone buzzes with a text from an unknown number.

> Interesting timing with your protest. We
> should talk. — DP

The air leaves my lungs. DP. Declan Pierce. Somehow, he

got my personal number—probably from one of the dozens of emails I sent his company over the past six months, back when I still believed in professional courtesy and proper channels.

"He's texting you?" Lianne's eyebrows shoot toward her hairline. "That's either very good or very bad."

Another message arrives before I can process the first:

DECLAN:

Perhaps we should discuss this face to
face. Coffee? Name the place.

I stare at the screen, thumb hovering over the keyboard. This feels like a trap, but it also feels like... what? An opportunity? A sign that maybe the corporate shark has a more human side than his fifteen-minute office meeting suggested?

"Maya?" Tito Ricky's voice cuts through my spinning thoughts. "What is it?"

I show them the messages, watching their expressions shift from confusion to concern.

"He's trying to open back-channel communication," Tito Ricky says. "Classic corporate strategy—divide the opposition by going directly to leadership."

But something about the messages feels different from corporate strategy. More personal. The casual tone, the acknowledgment of our timing, the fact that he bothered to text at all instead of having an assistant handle it.

Stop it, Maya. He's the enemy.

Before I can decide how to respond, the main hall erupts in voices. Through the office window, I can see more people arriving—families I recognize, teenagers from our after-school programs, seniors from the cultural preservation classes.

"Maya?" Lianne touches my arm. "People are starting to arrive. We should get out there."

"Give me a minute," I tell them.

After they leave, I sit alone with Papa's photos watching me from the walls and Declan's messages burning a hole in my phone. I type a response:

> I'm busy organizing a protest today. Rain check.

His reply comes almost instantly:

> DECLAN:
>
> I'll be watching the news. Try not to get arrested.

Despite everything—despite the fact that he represents everything threatening Highland's future—I find myself smiling at the message. There's something almost playful about it, like maybe the intimidating CEO has a sense of humor buried beneath all that expensive polish.

The thought unsettles me more than his coldness in the office did. Coldness I can fight. Humanity makes everything more complicated.

I shake my head and tuck my phone away. Highland needs me focused, not wondering about Declan Pierce's personality or why his unexpected humor sends unwelcome flutters through my chest.

I return to the main hall to find it transformed. Sixty-seven confirmed attendees has become nearly a hundred people clutching signs and wearing matching Highland

Community Center T-shirts. The energy is electric—three generations of community members united around saving Papa's legacy.

"Maya," Rosa appears at my elbow. "Channel 7 just pulled up outside."

Through Highland's front windows, I see the news van parking across the street. A reporter emerges followed by a cameraman already filming the crowd gathering on our front steps.

"This is it," Lianne says, appearing at my other side with that calm efficiency that makes her LA's most sought-after event planner. "You ready?"

I take a deep breath, thinking about Papa's legacy, about the families who depend on Highland, about the promise I made to protect what he built. Then I think about Declan Pierce, probably watching this unfold from his pristine office thirty floors above the city, and wonder if any part of him understands what we're fighting for.

"I'm ready," I tell Lianne.

And for the first time since this fight began, I actually believe it.

The march to Pierce Enterprises takes forty-five minutes through downtown's canyon of glass towers. We move like a river of determination, our chants echoing off the buildings that surround us.

"Save Highland! Save our community!"

I walk at the front flanked by Tita Sol and Rosa, with Lianne coordinating media interviews as we move. She handles the press with the same polished professionalism she brings to celebrity events, all charm and strategic messaging where I'm pure intensity and fire.

The Channel 7 reporter walks backward in front of us, her cameraman capturing every step.

"Thirty seconds, live," Lianne calls, waving me over.

I move toward the camera, mentally rehearsing talking points I've practiced for days. The reporter—young, blonde, professionally sympathetic—gestures for me to stand beside her.

"We're here with Maya Navarro, director of Highland Community Center, which faces demolition for the latest Pierce Enterprises development. Maya, what's your message today?"

The red light blinks on, and suddenly I'm speaking to all of Los Angeles.

"Highland isn't just a building—it's twenty years of community building. ESL classes for new immigrants, after-school programs for working families, job training, cultural preservation. Pierce Enterprises wants to replace our center with luxury condos none of our families could ever afford. We're marching to tell Declan Pierce that our community isn't for sale."

"What do you say to those who argue development brings economic growth?"

I look directly into the camera, thinking about Papa's dream and Declan's texts and the complex knot of anger and unexpected curiosity in my chest.

"I'd ask them to look at the communities where Pierce has demolished cultural centers before. Did those luxury developments hire local workers? Create spaces for existing residents? Or did they just push people out of neighborhoods their families built?"

The camera light blinks off, and I breathe relief even though the real test lies ahead.

As we round the corner onto Pierce Enterprises' block, the building rises ahead like a monument to corporate power. But I also see security guards forming lines and barriers being set up to contain our protest.

Of course they were expecting us. *Try not to get arrested*, he'd said.

"Maya," Lianne appears breathlessly at my side. "The Times reporter just told me Pierce Enterprises issued a statement an hour ago. They're calling this an 'opportunity for dialogue' and saying they remain committed to finding solutions that work for everyone."

I frown. That doesn't sound like corporate stonewalling. That sounds like someone thinking strategically about community opposition management.

As we approach the building, I find myself looking up at the thirtieth floor, wondering if storm-gray eyes are watching through those wall-to-wall windows. Wondering what Declan Pierce is thinking as a hundred people march through downtown's corporate canyon, demanding he listen to their voices.

My phone buzzes in my pocket—probably another text—but I don't check it. Not here, not now, not with cameras rolling and my community counting on me to stay focused on what matters.

Even if part of me can't stop wondering what he's thinking thirty floors above us, and whether his unexpected humor masks something more complicated than the corporate shark I've built in my mind.

The protest unfolds exactly as Tita Sol planned—orderly, passionate, completely peaceful. We set up across from Pierce Enterprises, our chants echoing off surrounding buildings. Media crews capture footage of seniors beside teenagers, three generations united in determination to save Highland.

It's beautiful. It's powerful.

And as I stand before the crowd leading chants and giving interviews, I can't shake the feeling that somewhere above us, the man who holds Highland's future in his hands is watching every moment of our carefully orchestrated revolution—and maybe, just maybe, starting to see us as more than obstacles to his development plans.

4

Declan

THERE ARE AT LEAST a hundred people standing outside the building, with onlookers gathering along the fringes. Of course Maya would pick DTLA rush hour to stage her protest. Judging by the TV vans parked on side streets, she's got exactly the attention she wanted.

Good for Highland. Terrible for Pierce Enterprises.

From my office windows, I watch Maya coordinate with what appears to be a small army of media personnel. She's traded yesterday's professional blazer for jeans and a Highland Community Center T-shirt, and somehow that makes her more formidable, not less. This is Maya in her element—not the polished activist who stormed my office, but the community leader who can mobilize a hundred people before most of the city has finished their first coffee.

The irony isn't lost on me. Twenty-four hours ago, I sat in this same spot wondering how to handle Maya Navarro. Now she's handling me.

"Sir?" Jessica's voice crackles through the intercom. "The board members are here for the emergency meeting."

I check my watch. Eight-forty-five. The meeting wasn't supposed to start until nine, but Harrison likes to get ahead of crisis situations. And a hundred protesters chanting outside our headquarters definitely qualifies as a crisis.

"Tell them I'll be right there."

My phone buzzes with a text from Maya:

> Rain check accepted. Don't do anything stupid while I'm busy.

Despite the chaos unfolding outside my window, I find myself smiling. There's something compelling about a woman who can organize a protest and send sarcastic text messages simultaneously. Which is exactly the kind of thinking that's going to get me in trouble with the board.

The conference room feels like a war council when I enter. Harrison sits at the head of the table with the other four board members flanking him like generals planning a siege. Stock futures glow on wall-mounted screens, showing Pierce Enterprises down another point in pre-market trading.

The sight of those red numbers reminds me why Harrison has so much power in this room. When stock prices fall, boards get nervous. When boards get nervous, CEOs get replaced.

Harrison doesn't look up from his tablet. "I assume you've seen the news coverage."

I take my seat at the opposite end of the table, as far from Harrison as the room allows. "Channel 7's been covering it live since six AM."

"The Times ran a front-page story this morning." Board member Patricia Winters slides a newspaper across polished mahogany. "Above the fold, with a full-color photo."

The headline reads: "David vs. Goliath: Community Center Fights Corporate Development." The photo shows Maya speaking into a reporter's microphone, Highland Community Center visible behind her. She looks determined, passionate, completely unafraid of the corporate giant she's challenging.

She looks like someone worth fighting alongside, not against.

"The story paints Pierce Enterprises as the heartless corporation destroying a beloved community institution," Patricia continues. "It mentions we've refused all attempts at dialogue."

"Which isn't entirely accurate," I point out. "I met with Maya Navarro yesterday."

"For fifteen minutes." Harrison's voice cuts through the room like winter wind. "And according to my sources, you spent most of that time letting her lecture you about community values."

Ice settles in my veins. Harrison has sources in my building—probably Jessica, possibly others. Which means every conversation, every decision, every moment of doubt gets reported back to the board chair who speaks with my dead father's voice.

"The meeting was informative," I say carefully. "I gathered intelligence about Highland's operations and their specific concerns about the Anderson Project."

"Their concerns are irrelevant." Board member Donovan Rice looks up from his phone with the expression of a man who's never been concerned about anything more pressing than quarterly earnings. "We have legal ownership, all permits, and a construction timeline that's already been delayed."

"The timeline was delayed for city planning requirements," I remind him. "Not community opposition."

"Until now." Harrison finally looks at me, his expression glacial. "Now we have protesters outside our building, negative media coverage, and investors asking questions about our crisis management capabilities."

As if summoned by his words, chanting drifts up from the street: "Pierce has millions, Highland has heart!"

"Catchy," mutters board member Melanie Doherty.

"Our PR team is fielding calls from three news outlets asking for comment," Patricia adds. "The kind where we explain why a multimillion-dollar corporation is bulldozing a community center that serves underprivileged families."

The words hang in the air like an accusation. Because that's exactly what we're doing, isn't it? Bulldozing a community center that serves families who can't fight back, can't afford lawyers, can't do anything except gather in the street with handmade signs and hope someone notices their pain.

Maya noticed. Maya organized. Maya made sure their voices couldn't be ignored.

"What's your solution?" Harrison asks, though his tone suggests he's already decided what that solution should be.

I think about Maya's fierce defense of Highland yesterday, about the incorporation papers scattered across my office floor like fallen dreams. About Harrison's systematic stonewalling and his threat to question my leadership if I don't fall in line.

"I propose we engage directly with Highland's leadership," I say. "Offer to collaborate on finding alternative solutions that address their concerns while protecting our investment."

The silence that follows could freeze hell.

Melanie actually laughs. "You want us to negotiate with protesters?"

"I want us to control the narrative," I correct. "Right now, Maya Navarro is writing the story, and we're cast as the villains. If we bring her to the table, we become partners seeking solutions."

"Solutions that still result in Highland's demolition," Harrison says flatly.

"Eventually, yes. But it gives us time to manage the optics while we handle legal and regulatory requirements. We look reasonable, they feel heard, and business proceeds as planned."

It's a cynical strategy—exactly the kind of calculated manipulation my father would have approved. Appear to make concessions while maintaining complete control of the outcome.

The thought leaves a bitter taste in my mouth.

"How long?" Patricia asks.

"A few weeks. Maybe a month. Long enough to demonstrate good faith while we finalize demolition preparations."

"And you think Maya Navarro will agree to this collaboration?" Donovan's skepticism drips from every word.

I think about Maya's intelligence, her refusal to back down, the way she organized eight hundred forty-three signatures while being systematically ignored. "I think she'll see it as an opportunity to explore alternatives."

"Alternatives that don't exist," Donovan points out.

"Alternatives we'll help her discover don't exist," I clarify. "By the end of the process, Highland will have exhausted every option, and Pierce Enterprises will be positioned as having gone above and beyond."

Harrison studies me for a long moment. Outside, the protesters have started a new chant, something about corporate greed and community needs. The sound carries through thirty floors of glass and steel—a reminder that Maya Navarro isn't disappearing quietly.

"One month," Harrison says finally. "You have one month to make this work. If it doesn't resolve cleanly, we move to more direct methods."

Something in his tone makes my skin crawl. "What kind of direct methods?"

"The kind your father would have used." Harrison stands, signaling the meeting's end. "Maxwell never let sentiment interfere with business necessity. Don't disappoint his memory, Declan."

After the board members file out, I'm left alone with the newspaper article about Maya and Highland. The photo draws my attention again—Maya speaking with complete conviction, unaware that thirty floors above her, six people in expensive suits were discussing her community's fate like a line item on a budget spreadsheet.

My phone buzzes with another text:

MAYA:

Hope your morning meetings went well.
The coffee offer stands when you're ready
to talk.

I stare at the message, wondering how she knew I was in meetings. Then I realize she probably watched the board members arrive. Maya Navarro pays attention to everything.

Which means she'll see through any manipulation I attempt. She'll know if I'm offering genuine collaboration or just buying time to destroy her father's legacy more quietly.

The thought should concern me. Instead, it's almost... refreshing. When was the last time someone challenged me to be honest instead of strategic?

I pocket my phone without responding and return to the window. The crowd has grown larger, with people spilling onto adjacent sidewalks. A police car idles at the corner—officers watching but not intervening. Maya has choreographed this perfectly: large enough to be unmissable, controlled enough to remain legal.

She's not just passionate. She's smart. Dangerously smart.

"Sir?" Jessica appears in the doorway with her ever-present iPad. "PR wants guidance on a statement, and Legal needs to know if we're pursuing injunction options."

"Tell PR to hold off until I've spoken with Miss Navarro directly. And inform Legal we won't be pursuing injunctions at this time."

Jessica's stylus hovers over her screen. "The board approved this approach?"

"The board approved my handling of the situation." Not exactly a lie, but not the whole truth either. "I'll be contacting Miss Navarro myself."

"Shouldn't that go through—"

"I'll handle it personally," I cut her off. "This requires a direct approach."

Jessica's expression tightens almost imperceptibly before she nods and retreats. I make a mental note to assume every conversation with her gets reported to Harrison.

Turning back to the window, I study the demonstration below. Maya has moved to coordinate with volunteers distributing water bottles. Even from thirty floors up, her competence is obvious—the way people naturally defer to her judgment, how she manages multiple conversations while keeping an eye on the bigger picture.

She's a natural leader. The kind of person who could run a company if she'd been born into different circumstances.

The kind of person my father would have either acquired or destroyed.

I pull out my phone and read her message again before typing:

> Meeting went fine. Are you free this afternoon to discuss collaboration opportunities?

Her response comes quickly:

> MAYA:
>
> Depends. Are you actually interested in saving Highland, or is this another PR strategy?

The directness catches me off guard. Most people don't ask such pointed questions in business communications, especially when addressing a CEO. But Maya Navarro isn't most people.

I find myself typing honestly:

DECLAN

I'm interested in finding solutions that work for everyone.

MAYA:

That's politician speak for "PR strategy." Try again.

Despite everything—the board's threats, the protesters outside, the millions hanging in the balance—I laugh out loud. When was the last time someone called me out so directly?

DECLAN:

Coffee at 2 PM? You pick the place. I promise straight answers.

MAYA:

Highland Community Center. 2 PM. Come alone, and wear something that won't make you look like you're slumming it.

I look down at my thousand-dollar suit and Italian leather shoes. Everything I'm wearing probably costs more than Highland's monthly operating budget.

DECLAN:

Understood. See you at 2.

The rest of the morning passes in a blur of meetings and phone calls, but my attention keeps drifting to the window. The protesters have settled into sustained presence, with people rotating while maintaining core organizers. Maya moves through the crowd like a conductor leading an orchestra, somehow making it all look effortless.

At lunch, I escape to my private bathroom and change into the most casual clothes I keep in the office—jeans and a polo shirt. It's still probably too formal for Highland, but it's the best I can manage without going home.

As I prepare to leave, my phone rings. Harrison's name appears on the screen.

"Second thoughts about this afternoon's meeting?" His tone suggests he knows exactly where I'm going.

"Just following through on the board's directive."

"The board's directive was to end this situation, Declan. Not to legitimize it by treating that woman like an equal partner."

"She organized a hundred people before breakfast, Harrison. Like it or not, she's already a player in this game."

"Players can be removed from games." The menace in his voice is unmistakable. "Your father understood that."

"My father's been dead for two years."

Silence stretches between us like a chasm. When Harrison speaks again, his voice carries the authority of decades spent wielding Maxwell Pierce's legacy.

"Be very careful, son. Some legacies are too important to let sentiment destroy them."

The line goes dead.

I stand in my office, looking out at the protesters still gathered below, and realize I'm at a crossroads. I can follow Harrison's path—manipulate Maya into believing we're collaborating while planning Highland's destruction behind her back. It's what my father would have done. It's what the board expects.

Or I can do something different. Something honest.

The drive to Highland takes fifteen minutes through

downtown traffic. I park across the street and sit in my car for a moment, studying the building that's caused so much upheaval.

Highland Community Center looks exactly like what it is —a converted warehouse painted bright yellow with murals covering the side walls. Children's artwork decorates front windows, and a hand-painted sign lists programs in English, Spanish, and Tagalog.

My father would have seen inefficient use of valuable real estate. Looking at it now, I understand his perspective. The building is old, probably not up to current seismic codes, situated on prime redevelopment land.

But I also see Maya's point. This isn't just a building—it's a community anchor, where people gather, children learn, families find support when they need it most.

Maya appears in the doorway before I can exit my car, as if she's been watching for me. She's changed from her protest T-shirt into a sundress that somehow manages to look both professional and approachable. Her hair is pulled back, and she wears the confident smile of someone on home turf.

I cross the street, and she meets me halfway.

"Declan Pierce, welcome to Highland Community Center." Her tone is formal but warm underneath. "Thank you for coming."

"Thank you for agreeing to meet." I gesture toward the building. "I have to admit, I've never seen Highland up close."

"Well, let's fix that." She leads me toward the entrance. "Fair warning—it's not as polished as Pierce Enterprises, but it's home to a lot of people."

As soon as we walk through the front door, I understand what she means. Highland hums with activity—children practicing dance moves in one room, adults attending what looks like job training in another, teenagers clustered around computers. The walls overflow with photos, artwork, and announcements in multiple languages.

It's chaotic and vibrant and completely unlike any space I've ever worked in. It's also undeniably alive in a way Pierce Enterprises' pristine offices never are.

"This is our main hall," Maya says, gesturing toward the large open area. "Community meetings, cultural events, emergency shelter. During the Northridge earthquake, we housed fifteen families here for three weeks."

We walk through the building, and Maya introduces me to people we encounter—Rosa, who runs the kitchen; Mrs. Hidalgo, who coordinates volunteers; Carlo, who helps with technology training. Everyone is polite but wary, clearly wondering what Pierce Enterprises' CEO is doing in their community center.

I don't blame them for the suspicion. If I were them, I'd be suspicious too.

"And this is my office," Maya says, opening a door at the back of the building.

The office is small but organized, with a well-used desk and walls covered with photos spanning Highland's twenty-year history. One photo catches my attention—a younger Maya standing next to a man who shares her determined expression and dark eyes.

"Your father?"

"Yes. Highland's tenth anniversary celebration." Maya's voice softens. "He would have been proud of today's protest.

He always said fighting for your community is never wasted effort, even when the odds seem impossible."

I study the photo, thinking about my own father's legacy and the expectations that shaped my approach to business. Maxwell Pierce would have seen Alejandro Navarro as naive, idealistic, doomed to failure in a world that rewards pragmatism over passion.

But looking at this thriving community center, at the photos documenting two decades of celebrations and achievements, I wonder if my father might have been wrong about some things.

"Declan." Maya settles behind her desk and gestures for me to take the opposite chair. "Let's talk about why you're really here."

5

___

Maya

As Declan settles into the chair across from my desk, I try to reconcile the man in front of me with the corporate shark I met last week. In jeans and a polo shirt, he looks younger, more approachable.

Almost human.

But I've learned not to trust corporate costume changes. Men like Declan Pierce don't accidentally wear casual clothes to community centers—every choice is calculated.

"I'm here because this morning's protest was impressive," he says, his gray eyes meeting mine directly. "A hundred people organized, coordinated media coverage, a message that resonated with reporters and viewers alike. That takes skill."

"Those people showed up because Highland matters to them," I say carefully, "not because I'm particularly skilled at manipulation."

The word choice is deliberate—let him know I understand what he does for a living.

"Don't sell yourself short." He leans forward slightly. "I watched from my office window. You moved through that crowd like you were conducting an orchestra. Everyone knew their role, everyone stayed on message, everyone looked to you for direction."

There's something deeply unsettling about the idea of him watching me from thirty floors up, analyzing my every move like I'm a chess piece he needs to understand before capturing.

"Were you taking notes for your security team?"

"I was trying to understand who I'm dealing with." His honesty surprises me. "Maya Navarro isn't what I expected."

"What did you expect?" I ask, though I'm pretty sure I know the answer. *Some hysterical community activist who'd fold under corporate pressure.*

"Someone easier to dismiss." A small smile plays at the corner of his mouth, but it doesn't reach his eyes. "Someone who'd accept a token gesture and disappear quietly."

I arch an eyebrow. At least he's being honest about underestimating me. "Many have made that mistake. It rarely ends well for them."

"I'm learning that." He shifts in his chair, and I catch a glimpse of something that might be genuine respect. "I certainly didn't expect someone close to my age who can mobilize a hundred people before breakfast and then send sarcastic text messages while running a protest."

Despite myself, I feel heat creep up my neck. *Focus, Maya. Charm offensive is still an offensive.*

"You started the texting," I point out.

"I did. And I'm glad I did, because it told me we might be able to have a real conversation."

"About what?" I lean back in my chair, crossing my arms. Body language that says I'm not buying whatever he's selling.

"About finding a solution that works for everyone."

Everyone. Corporate speak for "finding a way to get what we want while making you think you got something too."

"Define 'everyone,'" I say. "Because in my experience, when corporations say 'everyone,' they mean 'shareholders first, everyone else if convenient.'"

"Highland gets time to explore alternatives. Pierce Enterprises gets community cooperation while we work through the process. The media gets a story about collaboration instead of confrontation."

I almost laugh. "So Highland gets the illusion of a fighting chance while you use us as a public relations shield. Make it look like you're being responsive while you finalize demolition plans behind our backs."

"It's not—" He stops, runs a hand through his hair. "Okay, yes, the optics matter. But it's more than that."

"How much more?" I study his expression, looking for tells. "Because what you're describing sounds exactly like corporate damage control with extra steps."

"I mean that Pierce Enterprises is a business, and businesses adapt to changing circumstances. If the collaboration reveals alternatives that work financially, we'll genuinely consider them."

"Such as?" I keep my voice flat, unimpressed.

"Mixed-use development. Incorporating Highland into new construction instead of demolishing it entirely. Historic preservation that adds value instead of limiting it." He pauses. "I don't have all the answers, Maya. But I'm willing to look for them."

The admission sounds genuine, but I've been dealing with corporate doublespeak for six months. "What's Pierce Enterprises really getting out of this besides good PR? Because I doubt your board approved a collaboration just to be nice."

"Time," he says simply. "Time to let the media attention die down while we handle regulatory requirements. Time to explore options that might actually be more profitable than luxury condos."

There it is. "So it IS about managing the optics. Making Highland go away quietly instead of fighting you in the press."

"It's about business," he corrects. "But business that takes community impact into account. My father built Pierce Enterprises on the principle that profit justifies everything. I'm not sure I agree with that approach anymore."

I lean forward, genuinely curious despite myself. "Since when? Because your track record suggests otherwise. Three community facilities demolished since you took over, all replaced with luxury developments. That doesn't sound like someone who's questioning his father's approach."

Something flickers across his face—discomfort, maybe guilt. "Those decisions were made before I... before I understood the full impact of our development practices."

"And what changed? Some convenient corporate come-to-Jesus moment right when Highland becomes a PR nightmare?"

"Watching a hundred people march through downtown LA because they believe in what you're fighting for," he says quietly. "Reading eight hundred and forty-three signatures from people who trust you to represent their interests.

Sitting in this office and seeing twenty years of community history that my company wants to erase."

The words sound sincere, but I can't afford to believe them. Not when Highland's future hangs in the balance.

"Pretty words, Mr. Pierce. But actions matter more than speeches." I keep my voice steady, professional. "If we hypothetically agreed to this collaboration, what would it actually look like? Specifics, not corporate buzz phrases."

"Partnership. Joint meetings to explore alternatives, shared research on development options that preserve Highland's mission, coordinated community outreach." He leans forward. "Real collaboration, Maya. Not you versus us, but us working together."

"For how long?"

"As long as it takes to explore every viable option."

"And if no viable options exist?" I ask, though we both know the answer.

His jaw tightens. "Then Highland gets relocated with Pierce Enterprises' full support—funding, new facilities, assistance with the transition. No family gets left behind."

I want to laugh at the audacity. "You mean after you've exhausted every alternative and made yourselves look reasonable, you'll throw us some relocation money and call it charity?"

"I mean we'll ensure Highland's mission continues, even if the building changes."

"Highland's mission is tied to this community, this location, this building my father restored with his own hands." My voice hardens. "You can't just transplant a community center like it's a corporate office."

"I understand that. Which is why we need to explore alternatives that keep Highland rooted here."

I study his face, weighing every micro-expression. He seems genuine, but I've learned not to trust seems. "You want me to bet Highland's future on your good intentions?"

"I want you to bet Highland's future on a partnership that gives you more influence than fighting us from the outside."

At least he's being direct about the power dynamics. "And if I refuse? If Highland keeps fighting?"

"Then you'll lose," he says simply. "Highland is going to be demolished with or without your cooperation. The only question is whether you want to fight that battle from the outside or work for alternatives from the inside."

The bluntness should anger me, but instead it clarifies everything. He's right—Highland is outgunned, outfinanced, and running out of time. Six months of being ignored proved that traditional channels don't work. This collaboration might be my only chance to save what Papa built.

But it could also be an elaborate trap.

"If Highland hypothetically agreed to this—and I'm not saying we would—I'd need guarantees. In writing. With specific timelines, deliverables, and consequences if Pierce Enterprises doesn't hold up their end."

"Of course."

"And I'd need to know you have actual authority to make these commitments. I won't waste Highland's time collaborating with someone whose board can override every decision."

Something flickers across his expression—uncertainty, or maybe concern. "I have authority to negotiate. Final decisions require board approval, but they've authorized me to explore collaborative solutions."

Not a complete answer, and we both know it. "Your board authorized you to explore ways to make Highland's opposition disappear quietly. That's not the same thing."

"It's more nuanced than that."

"Corporate nuance usually means 'we're lying but with plausible deniability.'" I lean back, studying him. "Why should I trust you?"

The question hangs between us like a challenge. Declan is quiet for a long moment, and I catch something unguarded in his expression.

"Because you're right to be suspicious," he says finally. "Because everything you've said about corporate damage control and managing optics is probably true to some degree. Because I can't promise my board won't override decisions that cost too much money."

The honesty is more disarming than any sales pitch would have been.

"But," he continues, "you're also out of options. Highland can keep fighting and definitely lose, or take a chance on this collaboration and maybe find something that works. Those are your only choices."

I hate that he's right. Hate that six months of being ignored has led to this—trusting the enemy because it's the only path left.

"If I agreed to this—if Highland's board agreed to this— I'd need your word that it's genuine. Not a PR stunt, not a delaying tactic. A real attempt to find alternatives."

"You have it."

"Your word as CEO Declan Pierce who answers to shareholders, or your word as…" I pause, realizing I don't know who he is beyond the corporate title. "Actually, I don't know who you are as a person. Which makes this conversation even more problematic."

The observation seems to catch him off guard. "What do you want to know?"

"I want to know if the man asking for my trust is someone worth trusting. Or if you're just another corporate shark who's gotten better at hiding the teeth."

He's quiet for a moment, considering. "Person Declan Pierce studied public policy before his father had a heart attack and he had to switch to business to save the family company. Person Declan Pierce has been wondering lately if there are better ways to build something meaningful than the methods his father used."

"And which Declan Pierce would Highland be collaborating with?"

"Both," he admits. "But if you're asking which one would make the final decisions… honestly, I don't know yet. That might depend on what we discover through this collaboration."

Another honest answer that should probably worry me more than it does.

I look around my father's office—at the photos spanning twenty years of community building, at the awards Highland has won, at the calendar that shows programming booked solid for months we might not have.

Papa always said that sometimes you have to take calculated risks to protect what matters most. The question is whether this is a calculated risk or just desperation disguised as strategy.

"I need to discuss this with Highland's board," I say finally. "And with our legal counsel."

"Enrique de Leon. He has a good reputation."

"You've done your homework."

"I try to know who I'm dealing with."

Of course he does. Probably has a file on every Highland board member by now.

I stand, and he follows suit. "If Highland agrees to this collaboration—and I'm emphasizing if—I need absolute transparency. No decisions made behind our backs, no secret board meetings about Highland's future, no using us as cover while you advance demolition plans."

"Agreed."

"And if we discover you're playing games with Highland's future, the gloves come off. This morning's protest will look like a warm-up act."

Instead of being threatened, he almost smiles. "I believe you'd make good on that promise."

"Count on it."

He extends his hand across the desk. "Partners?"

I look at his outstretched hand, thinking about Papa's legacy and the impossible odds we're facing. About the community counting on me to save Highland and the fact that this might be our only real chance.

Or our biggest mistake.

I take his hand. "Provisional partners. Subject to Highland's board approval and contractual guarantees that protect our interests."

His grip is firm, warm, and lasts a moment longer than strictly necessary. When I look up to meet his eyes, I catch something there that makes my breath hitch—an intensity that seems genuine, almost personal.

Which is exactly the kind of thinking that could destroy Highland if I'm wrong about his motives.

"Maya." His voice is quieter now. "I want you to know this isn't just about managing a PR crisis for me."

"What is it about?" I keep my voice neutral, professional.

"It's about proving there's a better way to build something that matters. And it's about..." He pauses, seeming to struggle with words. "It's about not wanting to be the man who destroys something you've fought so hard to protect."

For a moment, I almost believe him. Almost let myself think that maybe Declan Pierce is more than just another corporate predator in expensive clothes.

Then reality reasserts itself. This is exactly what a skilled manipulator would say—appeal to my emotions, make it personal, make me think he sees Highland the way I do.

"I should walk you out," I say, stepping back from his proximity and whatever dangerous territory we're straying into.

"Of course."

We walk through Highland in silence, past children practicing dance moves and adults in afternoon classes. Declan studies everything—the artwork, the programs, the easy familiarity between community members who've known each other for years.

"It's not what I expected," he says as we reach the front entrance.

"What did you expect?"

"Something more institutional. Less..." He pauses,

watching teenagers set up for a study group. "This feels like family."

"That's exactly what it is." I follow his gaze. "Highland isn't just a building, Mr. Pierce. It's where people come when they need help, when they want to celebrate, when they need to remember who they are."

"I'm beginning to understand that."

We step outside into the late-afternoon sun. Pierce Enterprises' tower gleams in the distance—a reminder of exactly who I'm dealing with and what's at stake.

"Maya." He turns to face me. "This partnership—it's going to work."

"For Highland's sake, I hope you're right." I study his face one more time, trying to read the truth behind his words. "Because if you're lying, if this is just an elaborate way to neutralize Highland's opposition while you finalize demolition plans, I'll spend every day until that building comes down making sure everyone knows exactly who Pierce Enterprises really is."

"I understand."

"Do you? Because I'm not just threatening bad publicity. I'm promising a war you can't win quietly. Highland has eight hundred and forty-three signatures now, but if you betray our trust, I'll make sure we have eight thousand. Then eighty thousand."

Instead of being intimidated, he nods. "I'd expect nothing less."

I watch him walk to his car, every instinct screaming that trusting Declan Pierce is a mistake. But as he drives away, I can't shake the memory of how he looked when he talked about not wanting to destroy what I'm fighting for. Either he's the most skilled liar I've ever met, or there's something real underneath all that corporate polish.

Walking back into Highland, past Papa's photos and twenty years of community achievements, I realize I'm about to bet everything on my ability to outmaneuver a man who's been trained from birth to win at any cost.

The smart money says I'm walking into a trap.

But the smart money doesn't understand that sometimes the only way to save what matters most is to risk losing everything.

6

Declan

This is not how I usually conduct business meetings.

Yet here I am at eight in the morning, laptop open on a folding table that's probably older than I am, surrounded by the organized chaos of Highland Community Center coming to life. Two weeks of collaboration meetings have taught me that Maya operates on Highland time—which means community needs come first, schedules second.

I've been here four times in the past two weeks, each meeting lasting longer than the last. Yesterday's session ran until nearly dinner, and I found myself staying for Rosa's siopao just to extend our conversation about mixed-use development precedents.

Maya rushes in from her office, coffee in one hand and a stack of folders in the other, her dark hair pulled back in a ponytail that exposes the graceful line of her neck. She's wearing a sundress that would be completely inappropriate in Pierce Enterprises' conference rooms but fits perfectly in Highland's relaxed atmosphere.

"Sorry I'm late," she says, settling into the folding chair across from me. The movement brings a hint of her perfume—something light and floral that's been distracting me since our second meeting. "Tita Sol needed help organizing volunteers for tonight's cultural celebration, and Rosa wanted to discuss catering budgets, and—"

"Maya." I close my laptop and give her my full attention, something I've found myself doing more frequently. "You don't have to apologize for running Highland while we figure this out."

She pauses mid-explanation, and a smile tugs at the corner of her mouth. The same smile that's been haunting my thoughts during board meetings. "Right. I'm still getting used to the idea that Pierce Enterprises understands community centers have ongoing operations."

"Pierce Enterprises is learning," I correct. "This week has been educational."

That's an understatement. In two weeks, I've spent more time at Highland than in my own office—something Harrison has definitely noticed. His increasingly frequent "check-ins" about the collaboration's progress have gotten sharper, more pointed. More threatening.

"So," Maya opens one of her folders and pulls out a legal document marked with handwritten notes. "Tito Ricky reviewed your partnership agreement. He has suggestions."

I take the document and scan the modifications. Most are reasonable—clearer timelines, specific deliverables, protection clauses. But one addition makes me pause.

"A termination clause that allows either party to end the collaboration with seventy-two hours' notice?"

"His idea." Maya's voice carries a note of apology. "He

wants to make sure Highland isn't locked into something that becomes a waste of time."

"Fair enough." I make a note on my phone, hyperaware of how she leans slightly forward to read over my shoulder. "I'll have Legal incorporate these changes."

"Actually, there's more." Maya pulls out another folder, this one thick with research papers. "I've been looking into your mixed-use development suggestion."

She spreads documents across the table, and I find myself leaning closer to study them. Close enough to catch that floral scent again, close enough to notice the way she bites her lower lip when concentrating.

"This project in Portland," she points to an architectural rendering, "incorporated an existing community center into luxury condos. The developer got tax incentives for historic preservation, the community kept their gathering space, and new residents had access to cultural programs."

I study the rendering, noting the way the historic building anchors the modern tower rising above it. The design is elegant, profitable, and—surprisingly—something I could actually envision for Highland.

"What were the financial numbers?"

"Construction costs were about fifteen percent higher than conventional demolition and rebuild, but tax incentives offset most of that. Plus, the unique design commanded premium prices for residential units."

"You've done your homework." I look up to find her watching me intently, her dark eyes bright with anticipation.

"I told you Highland wouldn't go down without a fight." Her smile is equal parts challenge and invitation. "I just didn't mention that part of the fight would involve researching development strategies."

"You researched development strategies?"

"I researched everything. Mixed-use projects, historic preservation tax codes, community benefit agreements, affordable housing requirements—" She pauses, looking almost embarrassed. "I may have spent the last three nights reading zoning law."

"You spent three nights reading zoning law." I'm genuinely impressed, and something else I don't want to examine too closely. "Your boyfriend must be very understanding."

"Boyfriend?" Maya laughs, the sound echoing through the hall. "I don't have time for that. Highland takes all my waking hours, and apparently now my sleeping ones too."

She shuffles her papers, but not before I catch the slight flush creeping up her throat. The sight does something to my pulse that has nothing to do with business partnerships.

"No one special, then?" The question slips out before I can filter it through professional courtesy.

She looks up, and the eye contact lasts longer than it should. "I didn't say that. Just no one... current."

The air between us shifts, becomes charged with something that definitely isn't about development strategies. A pot clangs in the kitchen, breaking whatever spell was building.

"Anyway, I had help from Tito Ricky. And a lot of coffee." She pulls out another document. "I also found something interesting about the Anderson Project."

"What kind of interesting?"

Before she can answer, an older woman walks by with a

tray of golden-brown bread rolls. Without asking, she places two beside Maya's coffee and gives me a curious once-over before smiling.

"Salamat po, Tita Josie," Maya calls after her, then pushes one of the rolls toward me. Our fingers brush as I accept it, and neither of us pulls away immediately.

"You should try it," she says, voice slightly breathless. "She makes the best pan de sal in the city."

I take a bite, and the warm sweetness grounds me. "It's incredible."

"The kind where your luxury condos are planned two blocks from the new Metro expansion," Maya continues, sliding a city planning document across the table. "Transit-oriented development gets significant tax incentives and expedited permitting. But only if the project includes community amenities."

I study the Metro timeline while processing this information and trying not to think about how Maya's fingers felt against mine.

"The delays that spooked investors could actually increase the development's long-term value," I say.

"Exactly." Maya leans forward, excitement animating her features. "While other developers are backing away, Pierce Enterprises could position itself as forward-thinking. When the Metro opens, you'll have the only major development ready to capitalize."

The passion in her voice is magnetic. Everything about Maya Navarro is magnetic, which is becoming a serious problem for my professional judgment.

"And community amenities like Highland would be exactly what transit riders need," she continues.

I chew slowly, considering the implications while watching the way sunlight from Highland's windows catches the gold flecks in her dark eyes. "So you're suggesting we incorporate Highland into the Anderson Project as the community amenity component?"

"It would give Pierce Enterprises the tax benefits and expedited permits you need while ensuring Highland survives. Not just survives—thrives with proper funding and infrastructure improvements."

I stare at the documents, realizing Maya has handed me a development strategy that could save Highland while increasing Pierce Enterprises' profit margins. In two weeks, she's accomplished what my development team missed entirely.

"This is impressive," I admit.

Maya's smile is tentative. "So you think it could work?"

"I think it's worth exploring." I take another bite of pan de sal, using the moment to consider the political implications. "The numbers would need to work, and there would be questions about control, about Highland's independence."

And there would definitely be questions from Harrison, who's been increasingly suspicious about the time I'm spending here. But sitting in Highland's warm morning light, listening to children's laughter from other rooms, the thought of demolishing this place feels wrong in ways I didn't expect.

"What are you thinking?" Maya asks.

"I'm thinking it's a brilliant plan." I meet her eyes. "I'm also thinking this collaboration is getting complicated."

Her cheeks flush pink. "Complicated how?"

Before I can answer—before I can make the mistake of being completely honest—my phone buzzes.

"I need to ask you something," I say instead, setting the phone aside. "And I need you to answer honestly."

Her expression grows wary. "Okay."

"Do you trust me?"

Maya studies my face for a long moment. "I want to," she says finally. "But trust isn't something I give easily, especially to someone whose company wants to demolish my father's legacy."

"What would it take?"

"Time. And proof that you mean what you say about finding solutions for everyone."

"How do I prove that?"

She's quiet, her gaze drifting toward Highland's history photos. "Show me that Declan Pierce the person has more influence than Declan Pierce the CEO."

Before I can respond, laughter echoes from the main hall.

"Dance practice," Maya explains, checking her watch. "The teenagers are preparing for the Filipino-American Heritage Festival. Would you like to see?"

I should say no. I have meetings at Pierce Enterprises, investor calls, contracts to review. But the hope in Maya's expression makes the decision easy.

"I'd like that."

The main hall is full of teenagers gathered around a laptop, watching traditional Filipino dance demonstrations. Carlo Martinez waves when he sees Maya, then notices me and his expression grows uncertain.

"Carlo, you remember Declan Pierce," Maya says easily. "He's here to learn about Highland's programs."

"Are you here about the demolition?" Carlo asks directly.

Maya and I exchange glances. "Mr. Pierce and I are working together to explore alternatives," she says carefully. "We want to find solutions that work for everyone."

"Does that mean Highland isn't getting torn down?" A girl who looks about sixteen approaches, hope clear in her voice.

"We're exploring options," I tell her. "Nothing's decided yet."

It's honest, and judging from the way the teenagers' expressions brighten, it's more hope than they've had in months.

"Would you like to learn Tinikling?" Carlo asks. "We could use extra people to hold the poles."

I look at Maya, who's fighting back laughter. "Tinik... what?"

"Tinikling. Traditional Filipino dance," she explains. "Dancers step between bamboo poles that are rhythmically tapped together. It requires coordination, timing, and—"

"Trust," Carlo finishes. "You have to trust your partner to keep the rhythm while you focus on the footwork."

Maya's smile is knowing. "Perfect metaphor for collaboration."

Minutes later, I'm standing at one end of two bamboo poles, facing Maya across the space where dancers will leap between our rhythmic tapping. The basic rhythm is deceptively simple—tap the poles on the ground twice, then click them together once, repeat.

"The key is consistency," Maya calls out. "The dancers are trusting us to maintain the beat."

We start slowly, and I discover Tinikling requires more concentration than it appears. The rhythm demands focus while watching dancers leap between the poles, trusting them not to miss their steps.

"Good!" Carlo encourages as a younger girl successfully navigates the pattern. "Mr. Pierce, you're getting it!"

Maya laughs as I nearly miss a beat. "Focus on the rhythm, not the footwork. Trust that the dancers know what they're doing."

After twenty minutes, I understand why Carlo called it a collaboration metaphor. Success requires each person to focus on their role while trusting others to handle theirs. It's also surprisingly fun.

By the time practice ends, I'm laughing with teenagers who an hour ago viewed me as the enemy, and Maya is looking at me with something that might be approval.

"Not bad for your first lesson," she says as we help put away equipment.

"I may need practice before the festival."

Maya pauses in coiling extension cords. "You're planning to attend?"

The question catches me off guard. A week ago, the idea would have been absurd. But standing in Highland's main hall, having been included in dance practice despite representing a threat to their community, the answer is clear.

"If I'm invited."

"Of course you're invited," she says softly. "But fair warning—our cultural celebrations involve a lot of food, music, and people asking personal questions. Rosa's been asking about your family background since you started coming around. She wants to know if you're single, if you have children, and whether you can dance anything besides Tinikling."

Heat creeps up my neck. "What did you tell her?"

"I told her to ask you herself." Maya heads toward the storage closet. "Rosa doesn't believe in secondhand information when it comes to eligible bachelors."

"Eligible bachelors?"

Maya pauses in the doorway, her expression suddenly serious. "Declan, you should know that if you keep showing up here, people are going to assume you're interested in more than business partnerships."

"Are they wrong?" The question slips out, honest and direct and completely inappropriate.

Maya stares at me, and I can see her weighing how to respond. The silence stretches between us, loaded with possibilities.

"I don't know," she says finally. "Are they?"

Before I can answer, my phone buzzes with a text from Elliot:

> Board meeting moved to 11 AM. Harrison
> wants update on collaboration timeline.
> Where are you?

I check the time—ten-thirty. I've been at Highland for over two hours, and it felt like minutes.

"I have to go," I tell Maya, showing her the text. "Board meeting."

"Of course." Her expression shifts back to professional

courtesy, but something lingers in her eyes. "I'll email you the mixed-use development research."

I pause at Highland's front door. "Maya, about what I asked—"

"Focus on your board meeting," she interrupts. "We can talk about... other things later."

I drive back to Pierce Enterprises thinking about bamboo poles and traditional dances and the way Maya looked when she asked if Highland's community was wrong about my interests.

By the time I reach my office, one thing is clear—this collaboration is becoming far more complicated than I anticipated.

And Harrison is going to be asking questions I'm not sure I'm ready to answer.

The boardroom feels like a tribunal when I walk in at 10:58 AM. Harrison sits at the head of the table with the other board members flanking him, while Elliot Walker—my oldest friend and VP of development—offers a subtle nod of support from near the windows.

"Cutting it close, aren't we?" Harrison's voice could freeze summer.

I take my seat at the opposite end of the table. "Traffic from downtown was heavier than expected."

"Downtown." Harrison's emphasis makes the location sound like a moral failing. "Yes, let's discuss your recent fascination with that particular area of the city."

"The board authorized a collaborative approach to the

Highland situation," I say carefully. "I'm implementing that strategy."

"We authorized you to manage community opposition," Patricia Winters corrects. "Not to become their best friend."

"Four visits to Highland Community Center in two weeks, Declan," Harrison continues. "Care to explain why our CEO is spending more time in a community center than his own office?"

Ice floods my veins. Harrison's surveillance runs deeper than I realized.

"Effective management requires understanding the stakeholders involved."

"Understanding? Or something else entirely?" Harrison slides a tablet across the table. "Because this suggests your meetings with Maya Navarro have become quite personal."

On the screen is a photo of me and Maya during yesterday's Tinikling practice, both of us laughing as teenagers show us the steps. Someone at Highland posted it to social media with the caption: "Even Pierce Enterprises' CEO can learn new moves! Thanks for being part of our Highland family, Declan!"

Highland family. The words hit harder than they should.

"Community engagement is part of the collaborative strategy," I say.

"Community engagement or personal fascination?" Harrison's smile is razor-sharp. "Because what I see is a CEO who's lost sight of his responsibilities."

"The Highland collaboration has generated valuable development insights," Elliot interjects smoothly. "Maya Navarro's research could significantly increase the Anderson

Project's profitability while solving our community opposition problem."

I watch Elliot work, deflecting Harrison's personal accusations by reframing everything as business strategy. He's positioning himself as the voice of reasoned judgment while making Harrison look reactionary.

"Tax incentives and expedited permitting could save us months and increase profits," I add, following Elliot's lead. "It's a win-win scenario."

"It's a scenario that sets dangerous precedent," Harrison snaps. "Every community organization in the city will expect the same treatment."

"Only if we make it standard practice," Elliot says reasonably. "This could be positioned as innovative community partnership. Great PR, strong returns, and we avoid ongoing protest costs."

Board member Patricia Winters nods slowly. "Community opposition has been expensive on past projects."

Harrison's expression grows thunderous as he realizes the room isn't automatically siding with him.

"The numbers are irrelevant if our CEO has compromised his judgment," Harrison says coldly. "I'm seeing emotional decision-making where we need business strategy."

"What you're seeing is adaptive leadership," Elliot counters smoothly. "Declan identified opportunities where others saw only obstacles."

"Adaptive leadership doesn't explain why our CEO is planning to spend his entire Saturday at Highland's cultural festival instead of the Westside development site visit."

My stomach drops. The site visit—scheduled walk-through with city planners that's been on the calendar for weeks. Harrison knows exactly how this looks.

"The site visit can be rescheduled," I say, knowing how weak it sounds.

"Can it? The city planning committee specifically requested Saturday. But apparently, Filipino folk festivals take precedence over municipal relationships."

"Actually," Elliot jumps in, "attending Highland's festival shows Pierce Enterprises as community-engaged. Could be excellent optics with the city planners—demonstrates we work with communities rather than bulldoze them."

I watch Elliot masterfully turn Harrison's criticism into strategic advantage, but Harrison's expression tells me this confrontation isn't over.

"Fine," Harrison says finally. "The collaboration continues. But I want weekly updates and a firm deadline. Six weeks to prove this approach works, or we return to conventional demolition as soon as possible."

"Six weeks," I confirm.

"And Declan?" Harrison's voice carries unmistakable warning. "Don't mistake community engagement for personal relationships. This board won't tolerate leadership decisions driven by emotional attachments."

After the others leave, Elliot lingers behind.

"That was close," he says quietly.

"Harrison knows about Maya." I slump in my chair. "Someone's reporting back to him."

"Harrison has resources we're not aware of," Elliot warns. "Be careful. He's looking for any excuse to question your leadership."

"I know."

"Do you? Because attending Highland's festival tomorrow, after that confrontation, looks like deliberate defiance."

I think about Maya's invitation, about the promise I made to attend, about the way she looked when she asked if I was planning to come.

"Maybe it is," I admit.

Elliot shakes his head. "Then make it count. If you're going to risk your position for Maya Navarro, make sure it's worth the gamble."

After he leaves, I sit alone staring at the photo of Maya and me learning Tinikling. We look happy together, natural, like people who genuinely enjoy each other's company.

Harrison is right about one thing—my judgment regarding Maya has become personal. The question is whether I'm willing to bet my career on it.

My phone buzzes with a text from Maya:

> Festival starts at 10 AM tomorrow. Hope
> you can still make it.

I stare at the message, thinking about site visits and board expectations and the dangerous territory I'm entering.

Then I type back:

> I'll be there.

7

Maya

THE SMELL of adobo and lumpia fills Highland's main hall as I weave between tables laden with Filipino delicacies, checking last-minute details for the heritage festival. Colorful banners hang from the ceiling, traditional music plays softly in the background, and three generations of families set up displays showcasing Filipino culture and history.

This is Highland at its best—vibrant, welcoming, alive with community energy.

"Maya, anak, where do you want the lechon?" Rosa calls from the kitchen doorway, gesturing toward enough roasted pork to feed half of downtown LA.

"Main table, center position," I call back, then catch sight of Tita Sol directing teenagers in traditional dress toward the makeshift stage.

I check my phone for the tenth time in as many minutes. One-fifteen PM. The festival officially started at ten this morning, and Highland's main hall is crowded with families, community members, and half the arts district.

But no sign of Declan Pierce.

Which shouldn't matter. This is Highland's celebration, not some elaborate test of whether Pierce Enterprises' CEO will show up to eat Filipino food and watch traditional dances. The festival would be perfect with or without him.

Except I keep scanning the crowd for storm-gray eyes and broad shoulders, and I hate that I'm disappointed by his absence.

"Looking for someone?" Lianne appears at my elbow with a knowing smile, balancing a plate of lumpia and wine in a tumbler.

"Making sure everything's running smoothly," I lie.

"Uh-huh." Lianne follows my gaze toward the entrance. "And if Declan Pierce happens to walk through that door?"

"I will consider it proof that he takes our collaboration seriously."

"Maya." Lianne gives me the look she's perfected over ten years of friendship—the one that says she sees right through whatever story I'm telling myself. "You like him."

"I like that he's offering Highland alternatives to demolition."

"You like him," she repeats. "As in, you're attracted to the man who could save or destroy everything your father built, and you have no idea what to do about it."

Before I can deny her completely accurate assessment, Carlo Martinez rushes over with panic written across his face.

"Maya, we have a problem. The Cariñosa demonstration

needs more couples, and half our volunteers didn't show up."

Cariñosa—the traditional courtship dance that requires pairs to move through intricate patterns while maintaining eye contact and subtle flirtation. Beautiful, romantic, and absolutely requiring an even number of participants.

"How many couples do we have?" I ask.

"Three. We need at least five for the demonstration to look right."

I scan the crowd for possible volunteers. Most teenagers are committed to other performances, the seniors who know Cariñosa are busy with family, and middle-aged volunteers handle food service.

"Maya could dance," Lianne suggests. "She knows all the traditional steps."

"I'm coordinating the festival," I protest. "I can't abandon my—"

"Looking for a dance partner?"

The familiar voice makes me turn, and suddenly Declan Pierce stands behind me in dark jeans and a button-down shirt that makes his gray eyes look like silver. He holds a bottle of wine and wears an uncertain smile.

My pulse speeds up at his proximity. "You came."

"I said I would." He hands me the wine—expensive but not ostentatiously so. "I hope I'm not too late."

"You have perfect timing," Carlo interrupts, relief flooding his voice. "Maya needs a partner for the Cariñosa demonstration."

"Carlo—" I start to protest, but Declan already looks intrigued.

"Cariñosa?"

"Traditional Filipino courtship dance," Lianne explains helpfully. "Very romantic. Lots of eye contact and graceful movements that symbolize tentative approach between potential lovers."

I want to sink through Highland's concrete floor. "It's just a cultural demonstration. You don't have to—"

"I'd be honored," Declan says, his gaze fixed on my face. "If you'll have me as a partner."

The way he says "partner" sends heat spiraling through my chest. We're talking about a five-minute dance performance, but something in his tone makes it feel like a much bigger question.

"The performance starts in twenty minutes," Carlo says. "I'll show you the basic steps."

Before I can object, Carlo leads us toward a quiet corner where he demonstrates the Cariñosa pattern. The dance appears simple—graceful movements bringing partners close together and apart, hands almost touching but never quite connecting, eyes meeting and holding across the space between dancers.

"The key is the eye contact," Carlo explains. "Cariñosa tells the story of courtship through glances and gestures. The man approaches, the woman responds, they circle each other with growing interest."

I watch Declan absorb the instructions, his complete focus on Carlo's demonstration. When he turns to practice with me, his attention centers entirely on learning the steps correctly.

"Like this?" He moves through the pattern, his natural coordination making unfamiliar steps look almost graceful.

"Exactly. But remember, it's not just about footwork."

Carlo grins. "The story is told through how you look at each other."

Declan's eyes meet mine, and suddenly the practice session feels much more intimate than a dance lesson. There's a moment of awareness between us—an acknowledgment that we're about to perform a courtship dance in front of Highland's entire community while our professional collaboration hangs in the balance.

"Ready?" I ask, though I'm not sure I'm ready for any of this.

"Ready," he says, but his voice sounds softer than usual, almost uncertain.

Twenty minutes pass in a blur of final preparations, then Tita Sol announces the Cariñosa demonstration. The crowd gathers around the makeshift stage. I find myself standing in line with four other couples, traditional Filipino music beginning to play, very aware of Declan beside me adjusting his shirt cuffs.

"Relax," I murmur as the opening notes build. "It's just a dance."

"Right," he murmurs back. "Just a dance."

But as the music swells and we begin moving through the Cariñosa pattern, it becomes clear this is anything but "just a dance." The choreography brings us together and draws us apart in a rhythm that feels deliberate and meaningful. When the steps call for eye contact, Declan's gaze holds mine with an intensity that makes my breath catch. When we circle each other with graceful movements, the space between us feels charged with possibility.

The dance tells the story of tentative approach and growing attraction, and somehow, we're telling that story with our bodies, our movements, our eyes. The other couples fade into the background; the watching crowd disappears. There's only the music, the pattern of steps, and the way Declan looks at me like I'm the only person in the room.

When the choreography calls for the men to kneel while women dance around them with flowing scarves, Declan drops to one knee and looks up at me with such focused attention that I nearly stumble. When I brush the scarf lightly across his shoulders—the traditional gesture of tentative acceptance—my fingers graze his neck, and he shivers.

The final movement brings all couples together in the center of the stage, hands almost touching, faces close enough that I can see the gold flecks in Declan's gray eyes and catch the scent of his cologne. For a moment, the music holds us suspended in that space between approach and contact, and I'm acutely aware of the heat radiating from his body, his quickened breathing, the fact that we're standing so close I could count his eyelashes.

Then the music ends, the crowd erupts in applause, and reality crashes back.

"Beautiful!" Tita Sol calls out. "Absolutely beautiful! You two looked like you've been dancing together for years!"

I step back from Declan, suddenly aware we've just performed an intimate courtship dance in front of half Highland's community. The knowing smiles and approving nods around us suggest Tita Sol isn't the only one who noticed the chemistry between us.

"Thank you," Declan says, offering his hand to help me down from the makeshift stage. His fingers are warm, steady, and he doesn't let go immediately after I step down.

"That was…" I struggle to find words that describe what just happened without acknowledging how affected I am.

"Intense," he finishes quietly. "I wasn't expecting it to feel so…"

"Personal?"

"Yeah." His thumb brushes across my knuckles before he releases my hand. "Personal."

Before I can respond, Rosa appears with plates of food, and suddenly we're swept into the festival's social current—introduced to community members, offered samples of every dish, included in conversations about Filipino traditions and LA's changing neighborhoods.

Declan handles it with surprising grace. He listens when elderly relatives share immigration stories, asks thoughtful questions about traditional recipes, and makes everyone feel like he's genuinely interested in their perspectives.

"Your boyfriend is very nice," Tita Sol tells me as we watch Declan attempt to eat lumpia without dripping sauce on his shirt.

"He's not my boyfriend," I correct automatically.

"Hmm." Tita Sol's smile is knowing. "Does he know that?"

I follow her gaze to where Declan is helping Carlo's younger sister reach the dessert table, lifting her easily so she can choose between leche flan and halo-halo. The gesture appears casual, unconscious, natural.

"He's good with people," I observe.

"He's good with you," Tita Sol corrects. "I watched that dance, Maya. That man wasn't performing for the crowd."

Before I can ask what she means, Lianne appears with another glass of wine and a mischievous expression.

"Maya, Rosa wants to know if Declan knows any other traditional dances. Apparently, there's betting going on about whether he'll ask you to dance to the live music later."

"There's betting?"

"Rosa started it. Tita Sol doubled down. Carlo's running a pool on whether you two will end up together by the end of the collaboration." Lianne's grin is pure trouble. "I may have placed money on true love conquering corporate greed."

The live band—Filipino-American musicians who play everything from traditional folk songs to contemporary pop—sets up on the stage where we performed Cariñosa. Community members begin clearing space for social dancing.

"Maya!" Rosa calls from across the room. "Come dance with your young man!"

Every head in the vicinity turns toward us, and heat floods my cheeks.

"He's not my—"

"Would you like to dance?" Declan appears at my elbow. The band has started playing something slow and romantic, and couples are moving onto the improvised dance floor. Around us, community members watch with the kind of expectant attention usually reserved for wedding receptions.

"You don't have to," I tell him. "I know this isn't exactly your usual Saturday entertainment."

"Maya." He steps closer, close enough that I have to tilt my head back to meet his eyes. "I want to dance with you. Not because the community expects it, not because it's good for our collaboration, but because I've been thinking about it since we finished the Cariñosa."

The honesty in his voice makes my breath catch. "Okay."

He offers his hand, and I take it, letting him lead me onto the makeshift dance floor. The band plays something soft and lilting, with just enough rhythm to sway to. Declan's hand settles at the small of my back, warm and steady through the thin fabric of my dress.

"This is nice," he says as we begin to move together.

"Highland's festivals usually are." I'm hyperaware of everywhere our bodies touch—his hand on my back, my palm against his shoulder, the space between us close enough to feel his warmth.

"I meant dancing with you."

The simple statement sends heat spiraling through my chest. We're surrounded by Highland's community, swaying to romantic music under strings of lights that cast everything in warm, golden glow. It should feel like performance, like we're playing roles for our professional collaboration's benefit.

Instead, it feels like the most natural thing in the world.

"Declan." I look up at him. "What are we doing?"

"Dancing," he says simply.

"You know what I mean."

His hand tightens slightly on my back, pulling me a fraction closer. "I think we're figuring that out as we go."

The song changes to something even slower, and around us other couples move closer together. Declan follows their lead, eliminating the careful space we've been maintaining. Now I can feel the solid warmth of his chest against mine, catch the scent of his cologne mixed with lingering feast aromas.

"Maya." His voice is lower now, meant only for me. "I need to tell you something."

"What?"

"This collaboration—working with you, spending time at Highland, getting to know your community—it's changing how I think about a lot of things."

"Such as?"

"Such as whether profit margins are really the most important measure of success. Whether my father's approach to business was the only way to build something meaningful." He pauses, his thumb tracing a small circle against my back. "Whether I want to be the kind of man who can walk away from someone like you when this is over."

The admission hangs between us, honest and vulnerable and completely inappropriate for a professional collaboration. I should step back, remind him that we're business partners working on Highland's future, not potential lovers swaying to romantic music at a community festival.

Instead, I find myself moving closer, my free hand sliding from his shoulder to rest against his chest where I can feel his heartbeat, quick and strong beneath my palm.

"This is complicated," I murmur.

"I know."

"You're still the CEO of the company that wants to demolish Highland."

"I know that, too."

"And I'm still the woman who will fight you with everything I have if this collaboration doesn't work."

"I'm counting on it." His smile is soft. "I'd be disappointed if you were anything less than fierce about protecting what matters to you."

The song ends, but neither of us moves to step apart. Around us, couples transition to the next dance or return to conversations and food, but we remain still in the center of the makeshift dance floor.

"Thank you," Declan says quietly. "For including me today. For letting me be part of this."

"Thank you for coming. For learning the dances, for being patient with Rosa's questions." I pause. "For surprising me."

His smile is warm. "You've been surprising me since the moment you scattered those petition papers across my office floor."

I laugh despite the flutter of nerves in my stomach, and the sound seems to break whatever spell has been holding us in place.

"I should probably mingle," I say eventually. "Make sure everything's running smoothly."

"Of course." But he doesn't step away immediately. "Maya?"

"Yeah?"

"I'm glad I came today. Highland's community is extraordinary. I understand now why you fight so hard to protect this."

The sincerity in his voice makes my chest tighten with emotion. "I'm glad you came too."

Before either of us can say anything else that might complicate our professional relationship, Carlo Martinez appears with a camera and an eager expression.

"Maya, Mr. Pierce, can I get a photo for the newsletter? Tita Sol wants to document community partnerships."

I should say no. Photos of Declan and me dancing will fuel every piece of gossip and speculation already circulating. But something in his expression—hopeful, slightly nervous, like he's asking for permission to be part of our documented history—makes the decision for me.

"Of course," I tell Carlo.

Declan's arm tightens around my waist, and I rest my hand on his chest as Carlo snaps several photos. We're not posing for romance exactly, but there's intimacy in the way we stand together that will be obvious to anyone who sees the pictures.

"Perfect!" Carlo grins as he reviews the photos. "These will look great in next month's newsletter."

After he leaves, Declan and I remain standing close together. The festival continues around us—families sharing food, teenagers learning traditional dances, elderly community members telling stories about the Philippines—but I'm acutely aware of the man beside me and the dangerous territory we're exploring.

"I should go check on the kitchen," I say, needing space to process everything that just happened between us.

"I'll see if Tita Sol needs help with cleanup."

We separate, moving in different directions through the crowded main hall. But as I help Rosa organize leftover food and coordinate volunteer schedules, I'm hyperaware of Declan's presence across the room. I catch glimpses of him stacking chairs, carrying supplies, engaging in what appears to be serious conversation with Tito Ricky.

He fits here, I realize with a start. Not perfectly—his clothes are too expensive, his background too privileged, his world too far removed from our daily reality. But he's making an effort to understand, to contribute, to be useful rather than ornamental.

And that's more dangerous to my carefully guarded heart than any amount of corporate charm or strategic maneuvering.

8

___

Declan

It's six AM and I'm in my office, staring at the photos Carlo took at Highland's festival. In the pictures, Maya and I look intimate. Natural. Like we belong together.

Which is exactly the problem.

The past three weeks have blurred into something far beyond professional partnership. Evening computer classes where I help Highland's seniors while Maya coordinates programming. Late-night research sessions that turn into conversations about everything except development strategy. Shared dinners at Highland's community table, where Rosa treats me like family and Tita Sol asks pointed questions about my intentions.

Somewhere between teaching Mrs. Santos to video-call her grandchildren and helping Maya troubleshoot Highland's ancient heating system at ten PM on a Thursday, our careful professional boundaries dissolved completely.

And last Friday night, in Highland's storage room

surrounded by twenty years of community history, I kissed Maya Navarro like my life depended on it.

Now I have a board meeting in three hours where Harrison will expect an update on our "Highland situation," and I can't stop thinking about the way Maya felt in my arms, the soft sound she made when I pressed her against the shelving, the way she looked at me afterward like we'd crossed a line we can never uncross.

Because we had.

My phone buzzes with a text.

MAYA:

Morning meeting still on for 8 AM? I have the final financial projections ready.

Maya. Even her text messages make my pulse quicken, especially now that I know how she tastes, how perfectly she fits against me.

DECLAN:

Yes. Highland or Pierce Enterprises?

MAYA:

Highland. I'm already here working on the presentation materials.

Of course she is. Maya probably arrived before dawn, coffee in hand, putting finishing touches on research that could save her father's legacy.

DECLAN:

See you at 8.

I arrive at Highland to find the main hall transformed back into its weekday configuration—folding tables for after-school programs, art supplies for children's classes, computers for job training. But there are small changes I've started to notice—a new coffee maker Rosa insisted we needed, updated lighting in the conference room, my business cards sitting near Highland's front desk like I belong here.

Maya emerges from her office carrying folders and wearing jeans with a Highland Community Center T-shirt. Her hair is pulled back in a ponytail, and when she sees me, her smile is soft, intimate—different from the careful politeness of a month ago.

"Good morning," she says, and there's warmth in her voice that wasn't there before.

"Good morning." I want to kiss her hello, but Highland's main hall is already filling with morning volunteers, and we haven't discussed how public we're willing to be about whatever this has become.

"Coffee's fresh," Maya continues, settling across from me and opening her folders. "And I have everything ready for your board presentation. Financial projections, architectural renderings, timeline proposals—the works."

I note the slight shadows under her eyes. "Working late again?"

"Perfecting the research," she corrects. "Declan, this is our one chance to convince Pierce Enterprises' board that preservation makes business sense. It has to be flawless."

She spreads documents across the table—comprehensive financial analysis, detailed preservation timelines, architectural plans for mixed-use development. I force myself to focus on the numbers instead of remembering how her hands felt fisted in my shirt, how her fingers traced the line of my jaw when we finally broke apart.

"These numbers are incredible," I tell her. "Maya, this research is better than anything Pierce Enterprises' development team has ever produced."

"It has to be." Her voice carries the weight of everything Highland's community is counting on. "Historic tax credits, transit-oriented development incentives, premium pricing for authentic neighborhood character—every financial benefit increases Highland's chances."

I study the projections, noting how thoroughly she's addressed every concern the board might raise. But I also notice the way she bites her lower lip when concentrating, how her eyes light up when discussing preservation strategies, how she unconsciously leans closer when we review documents together.

Four weeks of collaboration have taught me that Maya Navarro is brilliant, passionate, and completely devoted to Highland's mission. They've also taught me that I'm falling for her with a certainty that terrifies me.

"Maya." I set down the financial projections and look directly at her. "I want you to know that I'm taking this seriously. Not just the research, not just the collaboration, but Highland's future. What we're building here."

"What are we building?" The question is soft, uncertain.

Before I can answer, my phone rings. Harrison Gordon. Calling two hours before our scheduled board meeting.

"I need to take this," I tell Maya, stepping away from the table.

"Declan." Harrison's voice cuts through the line like

winter. "I hope you're prepared for this morning's presentation."

"The Highland proposal is ready. Maya's research is comprehensive."

"Good. Because the board is growing impatient with this collaboration experiment. We need concrete results, not more community engagement reports."

"The financial projections show significant profit potential through historic preservation and mixed-use development."

"Projections are theoretical. What we need are timelines, measurable outcomes, and definitive decisions about Highland's future." Harrison's tone sharpens. "Declan, I need to ask you something directly."

Ice floods my veins. "What?"

"Are you maintaining appropriate professional boundaries with Maya Navarro?"

The question hits like a physical blow. "I'm focused on finding solutions that work for both Highland and Pierce Enterprises."

"That's not what I asked. Reports suggest your relationship with Miss Navarro has become quite... personal."

"My relationship with Highland's leadership is collaborative and professional."

"Is it? Because what I'm hearing suggests otherwise. And if your judgment has been compromised by personal feelings, the board needs to know."

I close my eyes, thinking about Friday night in the storage room, about the way Maya's breathing quickened when I kissed her neck, about how we've been pretending nothing has changed while knowing everything has.

"My judgment is sound," I tell Harrison.

"For your sake, I hope that's true. Because this board meeting will determine whether the Highland collaboration continues or whether we move to immediate demolition proceedings."

The line goes dead.

When I return to our table, Maya is pretending to review documents, but tension radiates from her shoulders.

"Bad news?" she asks.

"Board pressure." I sit down, running a hand through my hair. "They want concrete timelines and measurable outcomes."

"What kind of timelines?"

"The kind that end with definitive decisions about Highland's future." I meet her gaze directly. "Maya, I need to ask you something, and I need you to be completely honest with me."

"Okay."

"If the collaboration concludes that preservation isn't financially viable—if the numbers don't work—what happens then?"

She's quiet for a moment. "Then Highland fights. Legal challenges, bigger protests, public battles that make last month's media coverage look restrained."

"Even if it means destroying any chance of negotiated relocation assistance?"

"Highland's value isn't just financial, Declan. Sometimes you have to fight for things that matter, even when the odds are impossible."

Her answer is exactly what I expected and exactly what

Harrison fears. Maya won't back down quietly if our collaboration fails.

"What are you thinking?" Maya asks.

"I'm thinking that we need to make this work." I lean forward, lowering my voice. "Not just for Highland, not just for Pierce Enterprises, but because the alternative is a battle that will hurt everyone involved."

"And how do we make it work?"

"By giving the board something concrete. Timelines, financial projections, proof that historic preservation isn't just theoretical."

Maya nods, opening another folder. "Tito Ricky thinks we can get preliminary historic designation approval within two weeks if we file the right paperwork. That would provide legal protection while we develop detailed preservation plans."

"Two weeks." I consider the timeline. "Maya, I need you to understand something about Pierce Enterprises' board. They're not patient people, and they're not sentimental about community preservation. If we're going to convince them, we need overwhelming evidence that preserving Highland is more profitable than demolishing it."

"I understand." Maya's expression grows serious. "What do you need from me?"

"Complete financial transparency. Highland's operating costs, maintenance requirements, projected renovation expenses—everything. No surprises, no optimistic estimates, just hard numbers."

"You'll have them." She pauses. "What do you need from yourself?"

The question catches me off guard. "What do you mean?"

"I mean that Harrison's phone call obviously rattled you. And not just because of board pressure."

I study her face, noting the genuine concern in her expression. She's asking about more than business strategy. She's asking whether I can handle the personal complications of working closely with her while maintaining professional objectivity.

"I need to stay focused on solutions instead of..." I trail off, unsure how to finish honestly.

"Instead of?"

"Instead of thinking about kissing you in Highland's storage room. About the way you felt in my arms." The admission comes out rougher than I intended. "Maya, I need to be completely honest with you about something."

"What?"

"Harrison asked if I'm maintaining appropriate professional boundaries with you." I meet her gaze directly. "The truthful answer is no. I'm not."

Her breath catches slightly. "Declan—"

"I like you. More than I should like you, considering our situation." The word like is an understatement. After four weeks of collaboration that's become the best part of my days, after Friday night when she kissed me back like she'd been waiting for it as long as I had, I'm falling for Maya with a certainty that should terrify me. "And I think you like me, too."

Maya is quiet for a moment. "Even if I do like you, there's one glaring problem. You and your company want to destroy my community center."

"I don't want to destroy it," I say quickly, then pause. "I want to find a solution that works for everyone."

"But if you can't?" Her eyes are steady on mine, demanding honesty.

I taste the scent of fresh coffee and old wood that's become as familiar as my own office. "Then I have obligations I can't ignore."

Maya nods slowly. "I understand obligations. My entire life is built around them. To my father, to this community, to the promise I made when I took over Highland."

"So what do we do about it?"

Maya is quiet for a moment, her gaze drifting to where Rosa is setting up for the senior lunch program. "We do what we have to do."

There's something final in her voice that makes my chest tighten. She stands abruptly, gathering her folders.

"I need to grab some additional financial records from storage. The utility costs from last year—they'll help with your board presentation."

I watch her walk toward the back hallway, noting the tension in her shoulders, the way she's holding herself too carefully. Like she's fighting something. Like she's remembering what happened the last time we were alone in Highland's storage room.

I should let her go. Should stay at this table, review the documents, focus on the board presentation that will determine Highland's future. Should maintain whatever's left of our professional boundaries.

Instead, I find myself following her, drawn by the same magnetic pull that's been building for three weeks.

The storage room looks exactly the same as Friday night

—narrow space lined with metal shelving, single bulb casting shadows, twenty years of community history. But everything feels different now, charged with memory.

Maya stands with her back to me, reaching for a box on a high shelf, and I'm struck by how this mirrors last Friday—the same position, the same careful distance, the same electric awareness crackling between us.

"Maya."

She turns, still holding the box, and I can see in her eyes that she's thinking about Friday night too.

"Did you need something?" she asks, but her voice has gone breathless.

"Yeah." I step closer, close enough to smell her shampoo—something clean and citrusy that's been driving me to distraction for weeks. "I need to know something."

"What?" She sets the box down on a nearby shelf.

"When you said we do what we have to do—what did you mean?"

"I meant that we're both trapped by our obligations. You to Pierce Enterprises, me to Highland. And that maybe we're fooling ourselves thinking we can keep pretending nothing happened."

She trails off, her gaze dropping to my mouth before snapping back to my eyes.

"Maya." I step closer, close enough that she has to tilt her head back to look at me. "I can't stop thinking about Friday night."

Her breath catches. "Declan—"

"I can't stop thinking about the way you felt in my arms. The way you tasted. The way you kissed me back like you'd been waiting for it." I brush my thumb across her cheek. "Tell me you haven't been thinking about it too."

"This is dangerous," she whispers.

"Very dangerous." I lean closer, my voice dropping. "But I don't care anymore. I've been wanting to kiss you again since the moment we walked out of this room."

Her lips part slightly, and I can see the conflict in her eyes—wanting this but knowing she shouldn't.

"Declan, we can't—"

"Can't what?" I trace my thumb along her jawline, feeling her pulse quicken beneath my touch. "Can't admit that everything between us has changed? Can't acknowledge that this collaboration stopped being just business weeks ago?"

She doesn't answer, but she doesn't pull away either.

"I'm going to kiss you again," I tell her, my mouth inches from hers. "Unless you tell me to stop."

Instead of stopping me, she reaches up and pulls me down to meet her. Her hands fist in my shirt, and I press closer, backing her against the shelving exactly as I did before. But this time there's no hesitation, no careful exploration—just the certainty of wanting her and knowing she wants me too.

We break apart only when we need to breathe, both of us breathing hard.

"That was..." Maya starts, then stops, her fingers touching her lips.

"A mistake," I finish, though the word feels wrong.

"Right. A mistake." She nods too quickly, smoothing down her shirt. "We shouldn't have... I mean, we're supposed to be working together professionally."

"Exactly. Professional collaboration." I run a hand

through my hair, trying to ignore how she looks with her ponytail mussed, her lips swollen from our kiss. "This doesn't change anything."

"Nothing at all," Maya agrees, but she won't quite meet my eyes.

We walk back to our table maintaining careful distance. Maya spreads out the financial documents again, and I pretend to review them while stealing glances at her.

"So," Maya says, her voice overly bright, "the twenty percent historic tax credit should offset most of the additional construction costs."

"Right. The tax credit." I force myself to focus on the numbers. "That's a significant financial impact."

"Very significant. Completely changes the cost-benefit analysis." She's twirling her pen between her fingers. "Nothing else needs to change in our approach."

"Nothing at all. We'll proceed exactly as planned."

We sit in silence, both pretending to study documents while the memory of what just happened hangs between us.

"Maya," I start, then stop.

"Yes?"

"Nothing. Just... the research is excellent. The board will be impressed."

"Good. That's what matters. Highland's future."

"Highland's future," I repeat, though my voice sounds hollow.

Maya clears her throat. "I should get these final numbers compiled for your presentation."

"Of course." I gather my materials, grateful for the excuse to look anywhere but at her. "I should head back to Pierce Enterprises. Prepare for the board meeting."

"Good luck," she says, finally meeting my eyes. "I hope they see the value in preservation."

"They will," I tell her, though I'm not sure I believe it. "Your research is too compelling to ignore."

I stand to leave, and Maya walks me to Highland's front door—the same professional courtesy she's extended for weeks, except now I'm hyperaware of her proximity, of how she carefully maintains distance between us.

"Declan," she says as I reach the door.

"Yeah?"

"What happened in there..." She gestures toward the storage room. "It doesn't have to complicate things. We can keep working together."

"Professional collaboration," I agree, though the words feel like a lie.

"Nothing has to change."

"Nothing has to change," she echoes.

But as I drive back to my office, I know we're both lying to ourselves. Everything has changed. We've crossed a line that can't be uncrossed, acknowledged feelings that can't be unfelt.

I just don't know if we can pretend otherwise long enough to save Highland. Because at the end of the day, I don't even know if I can save it.

9

———

Maya

I'm still thinking about our kiss when my phone rings at two PM. The memory of Declan's hands cupping my face, the way he said he needed to know if what he was feeling was mutual—it's been replaying in my mind for hours, making it impossible to concentrate on grant applications.

His name on the caller ID makes my pulse quicken.

"How did the board meeting go?" I answer without preamble.

"Mixed results." His voice sounds tired. "Can we meet? I have information about the collaboration timeline, but I'd rather discuss it in person."

"Highland or Pierce Enterprises?"

"Actually..." He pauses. "Would you be willing to meet somewhere neutral? I know a coffee shop in the arts district that's quiet, good for private conversations."

After what happened in the storage room, maybe we both need space that doesn't carry Highland's history or Pierce Enterprises' corporate power.

"Is this about what happened this morning?" I ask quietly.

"We need to discuss the board meeting first. But Maya, we should probably talk about this morning too."

I take a deep breath. "Where and when?"

"Groundwork Coffee on Spring Street. Four o'clock?"

"I'll be there."

Groundwork Coffee is exactly the kind of place I'd choose myself—local, unpretentious, with mismatched furniture and local art covering exposed brick walls. Busy enough to provide privacy through ambient noise but not so crowded we can't talk freely.

I arrive first and choose a corner table, ordering a latte and trying to calm the nervous energy building since Declan's phone call.

When Declan walks through the door at exactly four o'clock, scanning the room until his gaze finds mine, my reaction has everything to do with remembering his mouth on mine and nothing to do with business meetings.

He's changed out of whatever he wore to the board meeting—dark jeans and a button-down shirt with rolled sleeves. The casual clothes make him look like the man who followed me into the storage room, not the CEO who has to justify decisions to directors.

"Maya." He settles into the chair across from me. "Thank you for meeting me here."

"Of course. How bad is the board situation?"

He orders an espresso from the passing barista before answering. "Harrison is pushing for accelerated timelines.

The board wants definitive decisions about Highland's future within two weeks."

"Two weeks?" My stomach drops. "That's not enough time to file for historic designation, let alone develop comprehensive preservation plans."

"I know. But we have construction contracts, investor expectations, and shareholders who are losing patience with community engagement processes."

I study his face, noting the tension around his eyes. "What aren't you telling me?"

"Harrison suspects that my judgment is compromised." Declan meets my gaze directly. "He thinks I'm too personally involved with you to negotiate objectively."

Heat creeps up my neck as I remember the intensity in his eyes right before he kissed me. "Are you?"

"After this morning, I think we both know the answer to that." His voice is quiet. "My judgment where you're concerned is definitely compromised."

"What does that mean for Highland?"

"It means I need to be extra careful to make decisions based on facts, not emotions. And it means I need to give you complete information, even when it's not what you want to hear."

"Such as?"

Declan pulls out his phone and shows me a financial projection. "The board approved one final collaboration meeting. You'll present your preservation proposal to the full board next Monday. If they approve moving forward with mixed-use development and historic designation, Highland survives. If they don't..."

"Highland gets demolished."

He nods. "Highland gets demolished."

I stare at the phone screen, processing the timeline. One week to prepare a presentation that will determine Highland's future. One chance to convince five board members who see community centers as obstacles to profit margins.

"What are my odds?"

"Honestly? Thirty percent, maybe forty if your financial projections are extraordinary."

"That's not very encouraging."

"It's realistic." Declan leans forward. "Maya, I want to be clear about something. I will advocate for Highland in that boardroom. I will present every argument, every financial benefit, every strategic advantage we've identified. But ultimately, this comes down to numbers."

The espresso arrives, and Declan thanks the barista without looking away from me.

"This is a lot of pressure," I say finally.

"Yes, it is." Declan reaches across the table, his hand covering mine before I can think to pull away. "On both of us."

The warmth of his touch sends electricity up my arm, and I realize we're holding hands in a public coffee shop, blurring every professional boundary we've tried to maintain.

"Declan." I look down at our joined hands. "What are we doing? Really doing?"

"I don't know," he admits, his thumb tracing across my knuckles. "But I know I can't pretend this morning didn't happen."

The gentle touch makes my breath catch. "We said nothing had to change."

"We lied." His voice is soft but certain. "Maya, everything changed the moment I kissed you."

I should pull my hand away, redirect our conversation back to Highland's presentation timeline. Instead, I find myself studying the way his fingers intertwine with mine.

"What would your girlfriend think about this?" I ask, fishing for information I'm not sure I want.

"I don't have a girlfriend." His response is immediate. "I can't, not when I can't stop thinking about you."

"You can't stop thinking about me?"

"Maya, before I met you, I'd spend evenings at gallery openings or charity events, usually with someone whose name I'd forget by morning." He pauses. "Now I spend my nights working on Highland research or thinking about our next meeting because there's no one else I'd rather be with."

The confession makes my chest tighten with emotion I can't afford to feel. "That's... that's probably not healthy."

"Probably not." His smile is rueful. "What about you? What do you do when you're not fighting to save Highland?"

"I go home to my apartment." The admission sounds pathetic. "I read, sometimes watch old movies. Work on grant applications. It's not very exciting."

"It sounds peaceful."

"It sounds boring," I correct, feeling heat creep up my neck. "I know it's not much—just a one-bedroom place in an old building. I could have bought something bigger, but I've been saving my money for..." I trail off, not ready to explain about Papa's life insurance money. "Other things."

"There's nothing wrong with saving money. Or with quiet evenings at home." Declan's thumb continues its gentle movement across my knuckles. "Where is home?"

"The Meridian Apartments. On Figueroa." I pause. "It's this old 1920s building—probably nothing like where you live."

Something shifts in Declan's expression. "The Meridian? That's the Spanish Colonial Revival building with the courtyard gardens?"

"You know it?"

"I know of it. It's actually on the National Register of Historic Places. Beautiful restoration work." His voice carries genuine appreciation. "Your apartment is in a historic building?"

"Third floor, overlooking the courtyard." I'm surprised by his knowledge of the building's history. "Most people just see it as old apartments."

"Most people don't understand that old doesn't mean outdated. Sometimes it means carefully preserved." His gaze grows more intense. "Sometimes the things worth saving are the ones with the most history."

The way he says it makes me wonder if we're still talking about buildings.

"Maya," Declan says quietly, "what are we really doing here? Because sitting in this coffee shop, holding your hand, talking about everything except Highland's presentation—this doesn't feel like professional collaboration."

"No," I agree, though I don't pull my hand away. "It doesn't."

"So what is it?"

I study Declan's face, noting the way the late-afternoon light catches in his eyes, the careful way he's waiting for my response.

"I think it's us trying to figure out if what happened this

morning was a mistake or the beginning of something we can't ignore anymore."

"And what's your verdict?"

I'm quiet for a moment, acutely aware of his thumb still tracing gentle patterns across my skin. "I think we're both in trouble."

"Good trouble or bad trouble?"

"I don't know yet." I finally pull my hand away, needing space to think clearly. "Declan, Highland's presentation is in one week. Everything I've worked for, everything my father built, depends on convincing your board that preservation makes business sense."

"I know."

"And you're telling me your judgment is compromised because of personal feelings for me."

"I'm telling you I'll advocate for Highland regardless of those feelings. But yes, my objectivity where you're concerned is questionable at best."

I lean back in my chair, trying to process the implications. "This is complicated."

"Very complicated." Declan finishes his espresso. "But Maya, complicated doesn't mean impossible. It just means we need to be careful."

"Careful how?"

"Honest with each other about what we want. Clear about priorities. Highland comes first—we both agree on that. But after Highland's future is decided..."

"After Highland's future is decided, what?"

"After Highland's future is decided, maybe we can figure out what this is between us without the pressure of professional obligations."

The suggestion is reasonable, logical, exactly what we should do. But sitting in this coffee shop, watching the way he looks at me, I realize that waiting might be easier said than done.

"I should go," I say, gathering my bag. "I have a lot of work to do before Monday's presentation."

"Of course." Declan stands as I do, pulling out his wallet. "Maya?"

"Yeah?"

"Thank you for being honest with me. About Highland, about this morning, about all of it."

"Thank you for advocating for Highland even when it complicates your life."

We walk toward the coffee shop door together, maintaining careful distance but hyperaware of each other's proximity. At the exit, Declan pauses.

"Good luck with the presentation preparation. If you need anything—research support, additional documentation, someone to review your talking points—let me know."

"I will." I hesitate, then add, "Declan? What you said about not being able to stop thinking about me?"

"Yeah?"

"It's mutual."

His sharp intake of breath is the only sign that my admission affects him. "Good to know."

"Good night, Declan."

"Good night, Maya."

I walk to my car while he heads in the opposite direction, but I can feel his gaze on me until I'm out of sight. Only when I'm driving home do I allow myself to acknowledge how much I wanted him to ask if he could see me tonight, how much I wanted to give him my apartment number instead of just the building name.

How much I wanted to stop pretending that what's developing between us can wait until Highland's future is decided.

But Highland comes first. Highland has to come first.

Even when my heart is starting to suggest that some things might be worth the risk of complicating everything.

10

Declan

My PHONE BUZZES as I'm leaving the coffee shop, Maya's scent still lingering on my clothes from when she brushed past me at the door. The memory of her hand in mine, the way her pulse quickened when I traced her knuckles, has my body humming with an energy I can't shake.

Harrison's name flashes on the screen.

> Can we meet? Off the record. There are things we need to discuss about your... approach to the Highland situation.

I stare at the message, feeling the familiar weight of corporate expectation settling on my shoulders like an expensive suit that's just a size too small. Harrison Gordon—my father's right-hand man, the keeper of Pierce Enterprises' legacy, the voice of shareholder responsibility.

The man who's been watching my every move since I took over the company three years ago.

DECLAN:

When and where?

HARRISON:

My club. One hour. Private dining room.

Of course. The California Club, where deals are made over aged whiskey and handshake agreements that reshape downtown LA. Where my father conducted business for thirty years, where tradition matters more than innovation.

Where Declan Pierce the CEO belongs, not Declan Pierce the man who's falling for a community organizer with fire in her eyes and petition papers in her hands.

Right now, I can only be one of those men—the one who can face Harrison and tell him exactly what he wants to hear.

Harrison is waiting when I arrive, seated at a corner table with two glasses of Macallan 18 already poured. He's dressed in his usual uniform—navy suit, Pierce Enterprises cufflinks, the kind of understated wealth that whispers rather than shouts.

"Declan." He stands to shake my hand, his grip firm and measured. "Thank you for coming on short notice."

"Of course." I settle into the opposite chair, noting how he's chosen a table where we can't be overheard. "You said this was off the record?"

"Indeed." Harrison takes a sip of his whiskey, studying me over the rim of his glass. "I wanted to speak with you not as Pierce Enterprises' board member, but as someone who worked alongside your father for fifteen years. Someone who cares about your success."

The words should be reassuring. Instead, they feel like the opening move in a chess game I'm already losing.

"I appreciate that, Harrison. What's on your mind?"

"Maya Navarro." He sets down his glass with deliberate care. "More specifically, your growing personal involvement with her."

Heat crawls up my neck. "My relationship with Miss Navarro is professional—"

"Son." Harrison's voice carries paternal authority that makes you feel twelve years old again. "I've known you since you were in college. I watched your father train you for this position. I can read the signs."

I take a drink, buying time while trying to figure out how much Harrison actually knows versus suspects. "What signs?"

"The way you talked about her during the board presentation. The fact that you've spent more time at Highland Community Center than in your own office this week. The reports I'm getting about your... collaborative approach."

Reports. Someone is feeding information back to Harrison, or someone at Pierce Enterprises is tracking my movements more closely than I realized.

"Highland's situation requires careful handling—"

"Highland's situation requires demolition and development, as originally planned." Harrison leans forward slightly. "Declan, your father built Pierce Enterprises on the principle that business decisions must be made with complete objectivity. Personal feelings cannot influence strategic planning."

"And if strategic planning evolves based on new information? If there are financial benefits to preservation we hadn't considered?"

"Then we evaluate those benefits objectively, without emotional attachment to the messenger." Harrison's expression grows more serious. "Declan, I made a promise to your father on his deathbed. I promised Maxwell that I'd help steer Pierce Enterprises toward the vision he'd spent thirty years building."

The admission catches me off guard. Harrison rarely mentions my father's final days, the cancer that took him too quickly for proper goodbyes.

"What vision?"

"To be the premier development company on the West Coast. To prove that strategic thinking and disciplined execution could build something that lasts." Harrison's voice carries the weight of old obligations. "Your father believed that business success required making hard choices, that sentiment was a luxury corporations couldn't afford."

"And if there are better ways to generate profit? If community engagement actually creates more sustainable revenue streams?"

"Then we pursue those strategies based on financial analysis, not emotional attachment." Harrison pauses. "Declan, Maya Navarro is an attractive, passionate woman fighting for something she believes in. That combination can be intoxicating to a man in your position."

The clinical way he reduces Maya to a strategic problem makes my jaw clench. "Maya is Highland's director. She's presenting viable alternatives that could benefit Pierce Enterprises."

"Maya is a community organizer who's very good at making her cause seem personal to the men she's trying to influence." Harrison's voice carries the patience of someone explaining obvious truths. "Your father faced similar situations—passionate advocates who believed that personal connection could override business reality. He learned to maintain appropriate boundaries."

"What happened?"

"Maxwell maintained professional objectivity. The development proceeded as planned, generated substantial returns for our investors, and established Pierce Enterprises as a serious player in Los Angeles real estate." Harrison's voice carries satisfaction mixed with something that might be regret.

"And the community leader?"

"Found other battles to fight. They usually do." Harrison checks his watch. "Declan, I'm not saying Maya Navarro isn't remarkable. I'm saying that remarkable women can be career-ending distractions if you handle them incorrectly."

Career-ending distractions. The phrase makes my stomach turn. "My career shouldn't depend on avoiding connections with people who challenge my assumptions."

"Your career depends on maintaining the judgment and objectivity that make you effective as Pierce Enterprises' CEO." Harrison's voice grows more intense. "I promised your father I'd help you avoid the mistakes that could destroy what he built. We can't let sentiment derail that progress."

"And if community engagement actually advances that progress? If Highland's preservation demonstrates that Pierce Enterprises can innovate beyond my father's model?"

Harrison sets down his glass and looks at me with disappointment. "Then you present those innovations based on financial analysis, not emotional connection. You advocate for Highland because the numbers support it, not because you're infatuated with its director."

The word infatuated hits like cold water. Is that what this is? A CEO's midlife crisis disguised as progressive business strategy?

But then I remember the way Maya's eyes lit up when she talked about her research, the intelligence behind her preservation proposals, the strength it took to fight for Highland's survival while planning for its potential relocation. This isn't infatuation—it's recognition. I'm drawn to Maya because she represents everything I wish I could be —someone who fights for principles instead of profit margins.

"Harrison, I appreciate your concern—"

"My concern is honoring the promise I made to your father." His voice grows more personal, vulnerable. "Maxwell trusted me to help you build on his legacy, not tear it down for romantic complications. I've spent fifteen years helping Pierce Enterprises become what it is today. I won't watch that success get compromised."

"And if it's both? If Maya and I share values that extend beyond Highland's preservation?"

"Then you pursue those values after the Highland situation is resolved. After you've proven you can make objective business decisions despite personal feelings." Harrison's expression softens slightly. "I'm not saying Maya Navarro isn't remarkable. I'm saying that remarkable women can be career-ending distractions if you handle them incorrectly."

He checks his watch. "I have another meeting, but I want

you to think about something—What would your father say about your handling of the Highland situation?"

Harrison's question follows me out of the club and into the early-evening traffic. What would Maxwell Pierce say about his son learning traditional dances and falling for community organizers? About boardroom decisions influenced by storage room kisses and collaborative meetings that feel more like dates?

He'd say I was weak. Compromised. Allowing sentiment to override strategic thinking.

He'd also say that business success requires sacrifice—that some things matter more than personal happiness.

But driving through downtown LA, passing the arts district where Highland sits and Maya works, I realize I'm tired of living up to my father's expectations. Tired of measuring every decision against what Maxwell Pierce would have done.

For three years, I've been CEO Declan Pierce, carrying forward a legacy that prioritizes profit over everything else. Tonight, I want to be just Declan—the man who's falling for a woman who fights for what matters, who challenges everything I thought I knew about building things of value.

My phone sits in the passenger seat, Maya's address programmed into my GPS from when she mentioned the Meridian Apartments. I shouldn't go there. I should drive home to my empty house in the Hills, review Highland's financial projections with professional objectivity, and prepare for Monday's board presentation without personal complications.

Instead, I find myself taking the exit toward Figueroa Street.

The rational part of my brain lists all the reasons this is a mistake—Harrison's warnings about appropriate boundaries, the board's skepticism about my judgment, the professional complications of getting involved with someone whose organization I might have to disappoint.

But the part of me that's been coming alive over the past month—the part that learned Highland community members' names and helped with cultural festival cleanup —doesn't care about rational arguments.

I need to see Maya. I need to find out if what's building between us is real or just proximity and shared goals. I need to stop being the CEO who makes careful, calculated decisions, and be the man who takes risks for things that matter.

The Meridian Apartments are exactly what I expected— modest, well-maintained, the kind of place where real people live real lives without pretension or corporate luxury. I park across the street and sit in my car for a moment, noting how different this neighborhood feels from the Hollywood Hills.

This is Maya's world. Community-focused, authentic, grounded in relationships rather than acquisitions.

Harrison's voice echoes in my head: *Career-ending distractions if you handle them incorrectly.*

Maybe he's right. Maybe I'm about to make the biggest mistake of my professional life. Maybe falling for Maya Navarro will compromise everything my father built, everything I've worked to maintain.

But sitting in my car across from her building, windows

glowing warmly in the evening darkness, I realize I don't care about maybe anymore.

I pull out my phone and type:

> I'm across the street from the Meridian Apartments.

The response takes forever—long enough for me to second-guess everything, to wonder if I'm making the biggest mistake of my career.

Then—

MAYA:

What are you doing here?

DECLAN:

> I needed to see you. But if you want me to leave, just say the word and I'll go. No questions asked.

Another pause that feels eternal. I watch the lit windows of her building, my heart hammering against my ribs like it did when I was seventeen and calling girls for the first time.

MAYA:

I don't want you to leave.

Relief floods through me, followed immediately by anticipation that makes my pulse race.

DECLAN:

> Unless you tell me your apartment number, I'm going to have to start knocking on doors. Starting with 3A.

MAYA:

3F.

11

Maya

As soon as I hit send, telling him my apartment number, I immediately drop my phone like it's on fire.

What did I just do?

I look around my apartment with fresh eyes—seeing it as Declan will see it in about two minutes. The mismatched furniture I've collected over the years suddenly looks shabby instead of eclectic. The stack of community center budgets on my coffee table screams "workaholic with no social life." The photographs of Highland events covering one wall might as well be a shrine to my father's legacy.

My heart races as I grab the budgets and shove them into a drawer. Should I change clothes? I'm still wearing the same jeans and blouse from our coffee meeting, now wrinkled from nervous fidgeting.

I catch sight of myself in the hallway mirror and try to smooth down my hair, then immediately mess it up again. Too obvious.

The knock comes exactly when I expect it, but it still

makes me jump. I freeze with my hand on the doorknob, suddenly paralyzed by the weight of what I'm about to do. Once I open this door, there's no going back.

My phone buzzes with Highland financial documents demanding attention. Papa's photo watches from the wall, reminding me that some things matter more than personal desires. Every rational part of my brain screams that this is a mistake.

But my hand is already turning the lock.

I open the door to find Declan standing in my hallway, his hands shoved deep in his pockets, his expression uncertain. The confident CEO who commands boardrooms and negotiates million-dollar deals looks almost nervous as he meets my gaze.

"Hi," he says softly.

"Hi." I step back, silently inviting him inside, my decision made.

He crosses my threshold, and suddenly my small apartment feels even smaller. His presence fills the space, making me acutely aware of how intimate this is—him in my home, surrounded by my life, no professional pretenses or neutral territory between us.

"This is where you live," he observes, looking around with genuine curiosity.

"This is where I live." I close the door behind him, hyperaware of the soft click of the lock. "It's not much, but—"

"It's perfect." He turns to face me, and the intensity in his eyes makes my breath catch. "It's exactly what I imagined."

"What did you imagine?"

"Warm. Authentic. Unpretentious." His gaze holds mine. "Like you."

The compliment sends heat spiraling through my chest. We're standing barely three feet apart in my small entryway, the air between us charged with the same electricity I felt in that storage room, in the coffee shop, every time we've been alone together.

"Why did you come here, Declan?"

He takes a step closer. "Because I needed to tell you something."

My heart pounds against my ribs. "What?"

"That I want you." His voice is low, rough with honesty. "Not just as a collaborator, not just as Highland's director. I want you, Maya. All of you."

The admission hangs between us, impossible to take back. I could deny it, redirect the conversation back to the presentation, maintain the professional boundaries that are already in tatters.

Instead, I tell him the truth. "I want you too."

His sharp intake of breath is the only warning I get before he closes the distance between us, one hand cupping my face exactly as he did in the storage room. But this time there's no hesitation, no questioning—just the certainty of his mouth claiming mine, hot and demanding.

I melt into him, my hands finding purchase on his shoulders as he backs me against the door. The solid thud of my body against wood sends a shiver down my spine that has nothing to do with impact and everything to do with the way his other hand slides to my waist, fingers splaying possessively across my hip.

"I've been thinking about this all day," he murmurs against my lips. "Since the moment I walked out of Highland."

I can't form coherent words, can only respond by pulling him closer, my fingers threading through his hair as our kiss deepens. He tastes like whiskey and desire, and the intensity of his mouth against mine makes me light-headed with wanting.

His hands slide along my waist, tangling in my hair, tracing the curve of my spine through my shirt. Each touch leaves a trail of heat in its wake, like he's mapping my body with deliberate precision. When his fingers slip beneath the hem of my blouse to find bare skin, I gasp against his mouth.

"Is this okay?" he whispers, his thumb tracing slow circles just above my hip bone.

"Yes," I breathe, arching into his touch. "More than okay."

He smiles against my lips, a flash of satisfaction that I feel rather than see. Then his mouth is moving along my jaw, down the column of my throat, finding the sensitive spot where my pulse hammers beneath my skin. The gentle scrape of his teeth there makes me clutch at his shoulders, a soft moan escaping before I can swallow it back. I should push him away, should maintain those professional boundaries I'm so desperate to keep.

Instead, I fist my hands in his shirt and pull him closer.

He groans against my lips, pressing me harder against the door. His tongue slides against mine, and I forget everything—the community center, our arrangement, all the reasons this is a terrible idea. All I can focus on is the heat of his body, the taste of his mouth, the way his hands slide down to grip my hips.

"Tell me to stop," he breathes between kisses, even as his

fingers slip under my blouse to stroke bare skin. "Tell me you don't want this as badly as I do."

I answer by nipping his lower lip, drawing a growl from deep in his chest. His hands tighten on my waist, lifting me effortlessly. I wrap my legs around him, gasping as he grinds against me.

"God, the things you do to me," he murmurs, trailing hot kisses down my neck. "I can't think straight when you're near me. Can't focus on anything but how badly I want you."

His words send liquid heat pooling between my thighs. I arch against him, seeking more friction, more contact, more everything.

"Then show me just how much you want me."

By the time we stumble into my bedroom, we're both half-mad with wanting. The door slams shut behind us, and Declan spins me around, pinning me against it. His lips trail down my neck, teeth grazing my skin in a way that makes me moan.

"I need you, Maya," he growls against my collarbone. "Now."

"Yes," I gasp, my hands fumbling with the buttons of his shirt. I need to feel his skin against mine, need to erase any space between us. He helps me, shrugging out of his shirt, his chest heaving with each ragged breath. His torso is a masterpiece of sculpted muscle, the planes and ridges of his abs glistening with a fine sheen of sweat. I run my hands over his chest, feeling the heat of his skin, the rapid beat of his heart under my palm.

His hands are everywhere, deftly undoing my blouse, sliding it off my shoulders. He pauses to admire me, his eyes dark with desire. "You're beautiful," he murmurs, fingers tracing the lace of my bra. I arch into his touch, craving more.

"Declan, please," I beg, my voice a desperate whisper. He responds by lifting me, my legs wrapping around his waist as he carries me to the bed, leaving a trail of discarded clothes in our wake.

As we tumble onto the bed, he kisses me deeply, his hands roaming over my bare skin, exploring every curve, every dip. I arch against him, feeling the hard planes of his body against mine, the evidence of his desire pressing against me through his boxers. His arousal is unmistakable, a hard length that makes me ache with need.

"You drive me crazy," he groans, his lips moving to my breasts, teasing and tasting. I tangle my fingers in his hair, urging him on, lost in the sensations he's creating. His fingers slip beneath the waistband of my panties, and I gasp as he touches me, his touch sure and skilled.

"Declan!" I cry out, my body trembling with need. He responds by sliding my panties off, his mouth following the path his hands have taken. I'm lost in a haze of pleasure, every touch, every kiss pushing me closer to the edge.

But it's not enough. I need more, need all of him.

"Maya," he whispers as he positions himself above me, his eyes locked on mine and I can see the raw need in his gaze. "I want you so much."

"I want you too," I confess, my hands gripping his shoulders. "Now, Declan. Please."

He doesn't need any more encouragement. He slides off his boxers, revealing his full arousal, hard and ready.

"Do you have protection?" I ask, my voice barely a whisper between ragged breaths.

His eyes never leave mine as he reaches for his discarded pants, retrieving his wallet. The moonlight filtering through my curtains catches the flex of muscle across his back, casting shadows that accentuate every ridge and plane. I watch, mesmerized, as he extracts a condom and tears it open with his teeth.

The sight of him sliding it on makes my breath catch. He's beautiful like this—completely exposed, vulnerable in his want, his eyes dark with desire as he returns to me. I can't help but stare, my breath catching at the sight of him. He positions himself at my entrance, his tip teasing me, and I arch my hips, desperate for him.

"Look at me, Maya," he commands, his voice husky. I meet his gaze as he slowly pushes inside me, inch by glorious inch. The sensation of him filling me, stretching me, is overwhelming. I moan, my nails digging into his shoulders as he seats himself fully inside me.

"You feel incredible," he groans, his forehead resting against mine. He starts to move, slow and deep, each thrust sending waves of pleasure through me. I wrap my legs around him, pulling him deeper, urging him to go faster.

He obliges, his pace quickening as he drives into me with purpose, each thrust hitting exactly where I need him. The headboard knocks rhythmically against the wall, keeping time with our gasps and moans. My hands roam his back, feeling the muscles flex and contract as he moves within me, the slick slide of our bodies creating a delicious friction that builds and builds.

"Maya," he groans against my neck, his voice ragged. "You feel so good. So perfect."

I can't form words, can only respond with breathless

sounds of pleasure as he shifts his angle, hitting a spot inside me that makes stars explode behind my eyelids. My body tightens around him, drawing him deeper, and I feel the telltale tension building low in my belly.

"Let go," he whispers, his lips brushing my ear. "I want to feel you come apart."

His words push me over the edge. I shatter around him, crying out his name as waves of pleasure crash through me. My back arches off the bed, my body clenching around him in rhythmic pulses that seem to go on forever. Through the haze of my release, I feel him watching me, his eyes dark with wonder and hunger.

"God, you're beautiful when you come," he breathes, his pace faltering as my body grips him tighter.

He follows me moments later, his hips jerking against mine as he finds his own release. The sound he makes— half-growl, half-groan—sends aftershocks rippling through me. His body tenses above mine, powerful muscles going rigid as he pulses inside me.

For several heartbeats, we stay locked together, his forehead pressed against mine, our ragged breathing the only sound in my darkened bedroom. Then he gets up and disappears into the bathroom. I hear water running briefly before he returns, sliding back into bed and gathering me against his chest.

The solid warmth of him, the steady rhythm of his heartbeat beneath my ear, creates a strange sense of security that I know is dangerous to feel. This is temporary—a release of tension, a moment of weakness, nothing more.

But as his fingers trace lazy patterns along my spine, I can't help melting into him, savoring the weight of his arm around my waist. Neither of us seems ready to speak, to break the fragile bubble of intimacy with words that might acknowledge what we've just done—and all its complications.

The night air feels cool against my heated skin. I should feel guilty or worried about what this means for Highland, for our professional relationship, for the presentation looming just days away. Instead, I feel strangely peaceful, my body humming with satisfaction, my mind quieter than it's been in weeks.

"What are you thinking?" Declan finally asks, his voice a low rumble against my ear.

I consider lying, offering some platitude about how wonderful it was—which wouldn't be a lie, but wouldn't be the full truth either. Instead, I give him the same honesty he's given me.

"I'm thinking about how I should regret this," I murmur, tracing circles on his chest, "but I don't."

His arm tightens around me. "I don't regret it either."

"That doesn't mean it wasn't reckless." I prop myself up on one elbow to look at him, taking in the way moonlight sculpts his features into something almost otherworldly. "Highland's future is still at stake."

"I know." He captures a strand of my hair between his fingers, twisting it gently. "But this doesn't change my commitment to finding the best solution."

"Doesn't it?" The question hangs between us, weighted with implications neither of us can fully dismiss. "You said yourself your judgment is compromised."

Declan's eyes search mine in the half-light. "Compromised doesn't mean corrupted," he says finally, his fingers still playing with my hair. "But Highland is the last thing I want to think about right now.

"That makes two of us," I whisper, though the words feel like betrayal to everything I've been fighting for.

His fingers continue their gentle exploration, tracing the curve of my shoulder, the dip of my collarbone, as if memorizing my body through touch. The intimacy of it makes my breath catch. This isn't just sex—this is something deeper, more dangerous.

"Tell me something I don't know about you," he says, his voice a low rumble in the darkness. "Something that doesn't involve Highland or work. Just you."

I consider the question, aware of our naked bodies pressed together, the vulnerability of being exposed in more ways than one. "I was named after what used to be considered the Philippine national bird, the maya. Well, until the national bird was changed to be the Philippine eagle."

"What does it look like, this... maya?" Declan asks as he pulls me against him.

"Small, like a tree sparrow," I reply. "Usually caught and sold in these little bamboo cages where they didn't do too well. My mother always bought them and set them free."

"You never told me about your mother."

"She was a preservationist too, in her own way." I smile against his chest, memories washing over me in the dim light. "Not of buildings, but of traditions, stories. She taught Filipino folklore at the university—spent her life documenting oral histories that might otherwise have disappeared."

"Is that where you got it from? The need to preserve what matters?"

I consider this, tracing idle patterns across his skin. "Maybe. She always said that once something's gone, you can't get it back—not really. You can rebuild, recreate, but the soul of the original is lost." I pause, realizing how much this explains about my fight for Highland. "She died when I was in high school. Cancer. My father dedicated Highland's classroom to her."

Declan's hand stills against my back, then resumes its gentle stroking. "I'm sorry."

"It was a long time ago." The familiar ache is there, but dulled by time. "What about you? Tell me something I don't know about Declan Pierce."

He's quiet for so long I wonder if he's fallen asleep. Then he shifts, pulling me closer against the solid warmth of his chest. "My mother left us when I was seven."

The admission hangs in the air, his voice carrying a detachment that feels practiced, as if he's learned to say the words without feeling them. I wait, giving him space to continue or retreat.

"She decided corporate life wasn't for her," he says finally. "My father was building Pierce Enterprises, working eighty-hour weeks. She wanted something... simpler."

"Where did she go?" I ask softly, my fingers tracing the contours of his chest.

"New Mexico, initially. Then Colorado. She moved around, following whatever spiritual path caught her interest." There's a controlled neutrality in his tone that tells me more than his words. "She sent birthday cards for a few years, then Christmas cards, then nothing."

I press my lips against his shoulder, a wordless comfort

for a wound I can tell has never fully healed. "Did you ever see her again?"

"Once, when I was in college." His voice is distant now, as if he's recalling something he keeps carefully locked away. "I tracked her down to this commune in New Mexico. She was living in a yurt, making pottery and teaching meditation to tourists."

I stay quiet, feeling the tension in his body as he speaks.

"She seemed happy to see me, but it was like meeting a stranger. Someone who happened to have my eyes and knew details about my childhood." His fingers trace idle patterns on my bare shoulder. "She asked if I was still playing baseball. I hadn't played since eighth grade."

The sadness in his voice makes my chest ache. I press closer to him, offering wordless comfort.

"My father never remarried. Just threw himself into the business. Pierce Enterprises became his entire identity." Declan's chest rises and falls with a deep breath. "I suppose that's why he expected I'd follow in his footsteps. Take over the company and take it to new heights. Build the Pierce legacy."

"Is that what you wanted?" I ask, hearing the echo of expectation in his words.

He's quiet for a moment, his fingers continuing their gentle exploration of my skin. "I wanted to make him proud," he finally says. "After my mother left, that became... everything."

I lift my head to look at him, finding his eyes in the moonlight. There's vulnerability there I've never seen before —not in the boardroom, not during our negotiations, not even when he kissed me in the storage room.

"And now?" I whisper, knowing I'm asking about more than just his relationship with his father.

"Now I'm lying in bed with a woman who challenges everything I thought I knew about what I want." His hand cups my face, thumb tracing my lower lip. "A woman who fights for what matters to her with a ferocity that makes me question what I'm fighting for."

"Is that good or bad?"

"I don't know yet," he replies. "But I know I want to find out."

He kisses me then, slow and deep, his hand sliding into my hair to cradle my head. This kiss is different from our earlier urgency—deliberate, exploratory, like he's trying to memorize the taste and feel of me. I melt into him, my body responding with a languid heat that builds slowly from my core outward.

When he pulls away, his eyes are dark pools of desire in the moonlight. "It's late," he murmurs, but makes no move to leave, his hand tracing the curve of my hip and sending shivers across my skin.

"Stay," I whisper, surprising myself with how much I want him to. How much I need the warmth of his body next to mine tonight.

Maybe because I know in the morning, everything will be different. In the harsh light of day, we'll have to face the consequences of what we've done. The way we've complicated an already precarious situation. The lines we've crossed that can never be uncrossed.

But tonight, in the soft darkness of my bedroom, I want to pretend those complications don't exist.

"Are you sure?" he asks, his voice rough with something that sounds like hope.

I answer by pulling him closer, my lips finding his in the darkness. His response is immediate, arms tightening around me as he rolls me beneath him. This time there's no urgency, no desperate rush—just the slow, deliberate exploration of bodies learning each other's secrets.

At least, for tonight.

12

Declan

I CAN'T FOCUS on a damn thing. The quarterly reports blur in front of me as my mind drifts back to last night—to Maya. The way she felt beneath me, the sounds she made, how perfectly she fit in my arms. I wanted to stay till morning, wake her up with kisses and another round of what we'd done in the dark. But reality has sharp edges that cut through fantasies.

I left before dawn, watching her sleep for one selfish minute before slipping out, the floorboards creaking a quiet accusation beneath my feet.

And then there was her text—

> Now things can go back to normal.

Normal. As in, fake.

As in, I don't get to touch her, taste her, have her beneath me, sighing my name...

I close my eyes, running a hand over my face. This is bad.

Really fucking bad.

The intercom buzzes. "Mr. Pierce? Mr. Walker is here to see you."

Perfect. Just what I need. "Send him in."

Normally, Elliot would just waltz in which tells me he wants this entrance to make a point.

"Well, well, well. You look like hell," he says as he strolls in like he owns the place and drops into one of my leather chairs with a knowing smirk. I swear one day he'll end up sitting in my chair—and unlike me, he'll actually deserve it. I inherited this position because my last name is Pierce. Elliot's been earning it every day for the past six years.

"Thanks." I turn back to my computer, trying to at least pretend I'm working.

"Late night?" His tone is innocent. Too innocent.

I shoot him a warning look. "Don't start."

"What? Can't a guy check on his best friend?" He leans forward, grinning. "Especially when said best friend was seen visiting the apartment of a certain stunning brunette community advocate."

I turn to face him. "You're having me followed now?"

"Oh please." Elliot waves his hand dismissively. "Mrs. Foster from 4B called me this morning. She's on the board of that literacy foundation we fund. Apparently, she was walking her dog when you did your little walk of shame at 5 AM. At least, she thinks it was you."

The office suddenly feels too small, the air too thin. I swivel my chair toward the floor-to-ceiling windows, the city of Los Angeles sprawled below me.

Walk of shame, my ass. I haven't done a walk of shame in years.

"It wasn't like that," I mutter even though it absolutely was.

Elliot doesn't say anything for a few moments, his eyes narrowing as he studies me. "You've got it bad, man."

"I don't 'got' anything." I stand up, needing to move. The morning sun bathes the city below in a silver haze, revealing a clear view all the way to Santa Monica.

"Right," Elliot says, drawing out the word. "And I'm the King of England."

I turn to face him, my jaw clenched. "It was just sex, El. A one-time thing to get it out of our systems."

"How's that working out for you?" His voice holds no mockery now, just genuine concern.

The truth burns in my throat. I want to say it worked perfectly, that I'm fine, that Maya is just another woman who's passing through my life. But the lie won't form.

Instead, I know I have to lie to her. Eventually. I have to tell her that all the work we've been doing won't produce the outcome she wants.

Instead, it will produce the outcome Pierce Enterprises has already invested millions in securing. That I can't stop the development that will destroy her community center, and it will be torn down with the rest of her block.

"Earth to Declan," Elliot says, "Where'd you go just now?"

"Nowhere good." I square my shoulders, pulling myself back to the present. "Anyway, it's complicated."

"Only because you're making it complicated." Elliot's voice turns serious. "I've known you since college, Dec. I've never seen you like this about anyone."

I press my forehead against the cool glass. "She deserves better than me."

"Better than the CEO who's clearly crazy about her?"

"Better than someone who's spent years being exactly what she hates—a corporate shark who puts profits over people." I turn back to face him. "You should hear the way she talks about community, Elliot, about making a real difference. She sees right through all this." I gesture at my office, the trappings of wealth and power that used to mean everything.

"So prove her wrong." Elliot shrugs like it's the simplest thing in the world. "Show her who you really are."

"And who's that? The man who'll go back on his word to her community just to please the board? The man who's been lying to her face for weeks?" I push away from the window, the knot in my stomach tightening. "I'm exactly who she thinks I am."

"That's bullshit and you know it." Elliot stands, his casual demeanor gone. "You've been looking for a way out of this development deal since before you met her."

I run my hand through my hair, feeling the strands stick up in defiance. "Looking for a way out and finding one are two different things. The board votes next week."

And then there's Harrison. But I don't need to tell Elliot that.

"So find a solution before then." He steps closer, lowering his voice though we're alone. "I've seen the alternative proposals. They're solid."

The alternative proposals. My secret project for the past few weeks—ways to develop the area without demolishing the community center. Ways that would still turn a profit—

just not the obscene margins that Pierce Enterprises is known for. The numbers are tight but workable, especially if I can convince a few key investors to back the more community-focused approach.

"The board will never go for it," I say, but there's less conviction in my voice than there was a week ago.

"Maybe. Maybe not." Elliot leans against my desk. "But at least you'd be able to look her in the eye again."

The thought of Maya's eyes—those deep-brown pools that seem to see straight through to the parts of me I've spent years burying—makes my chest ache. Last night, when she looked up at me, her body arching into mine, I saw something there beyond desire. Trust.

The irony isn't lost on me.

My phone vibrates against the desk. Maya's name flashes across the screen, and my heart does a traitorous little leap. I stare at her name, transfixed, as if the letters themselves might offer some clue to what she's thinking.

"Aren't you going to answer that?" Elliot asks, eyebrows raised.

I swipe the notification away. "Later."

"Coward."

"Strategic," I counter, but the word tastes sour. "I need to figure out what I'm going to say to her first."

"How about the truth?" Elliot suggests, his voice gentler than I deserve.

The truth. Such a simple concept, yet so impossible in execution. The truth would mean admitting I've been playing both sides from the beginning. That every time we've met to discuss "community input" on the development, I've been feeding her half-truths, knowing full well the decision was practically made before we ever shook hands.

"It's not that simple."

"Isn't it?" Elliot heads for the door, pausing with his hand on the handle. "You know, for someone so smart, you can be incredibly dense. That woman looks at you the same way you look at her."

"Elliot—"

"Just think about it. And for what it's worth, I think you're a better man than you give yourself credit for," he says before closing the door behind him, leaving me alone with thoughts that feel too big for my office, too real for the sanitized corporate world I've built around myself.

I stare at my phone again. Maya's message sits there, unopened. One tap and I'd see her words, hear her voice in my head. But I'm not ready. Not when my mind keeps circling back to the way she felt in my arms, the vulnerability in her eyes when she whispered against my lips, "I shouldn't want you this much."

The truth is, I shouldn't want her either. Not when I'm holding the blade that could cut through everything she's built.

I pick up the phone, then set it down again. The city sprawls before me, a concrete maze of ambition and compromise. Somewhere out there, Maya is going about her day, maybe thinking of last night, maybe regretting it. Maybe waiting for me to respond.

My computer pings with an email from Harrison. I don't need to open it to know what it says. Another thinly veiled threat wrapped in corporate speak, reminding me of my duty to the shareholders, to the Pierce legacy. My father's right-hand man turned my personal shadow, making sure I don't stray too far from the path that's been laid out for me since birth.

I swipe the notification away, the feeling of dull resignation settling in my bones like an old friend. I'm suddenly struck by how tired I am of this—of the game, the constant chess match between shareholders' expectations and my own increasingly murky sense of right.

My phone buzzes with a text from Maya—

MAYA:

Thank you for last night. For everything. I'm working on those financial projections for the board presentation. This could actually work.

The optimism in her message makes my chest ache. She believes in this collaboration. She believes the board will listen to reason, that her research and passion can overcome decades of Pierce Enterprises' profit-first mentality.

She believes in me.

I think about Harrison's warning, about maintaining professional boundaries. About the board's impatience and their willingness to steamroll over Highland if this collaboration doesn't produce results quickly.

Another text arrives—

MAYA:

Question about the historic tax credit calculations—can we set up a call later? I want to make sure the numbers are bulletproof.

Bulletproof. As if numbers and logic could protect Highland from five board members who see community centers as obstacles to quarterly profits.

I draft three different responses, deleting each one.

What am I supposed to tell her? That Harrison suspects our relationship? That the board is looking for any excuse to end this collaboration? That even with perfect financial projections, Highland's chances are maybe thirty percent at best?

That I spent the night in her bed while knowing I might have to choose between her and everything I've built my life around?

Elliot's words echo in my mind—*Show her who you really are.* But what if who I really am is someone who disappoints the people he cares about? What if the corporate shark Maya initially saw is the truest version of myself?

My father never would have gotten emotionally involved with someone on the opposite side of a business deal. Maxwell Pierce compartmentalized everything—personal feelings never interfered with strategic decisions. That's how he built Pierce Enterprises into a company that matters.

I finally text back—

DECLAN:

Let's discuss tonight. Dinner?

Her response comes immediately.

MAYA:

My place? I'll cook. Fair warning—it won't
be as fancy as whatever you're used to.

I stare at her message, thinking about her small apartment with its mismatched furniture and community center photos covering the walls. The warmth and authenticity of a space that tells the story of who she is.

DECLAN:

Actually, let me cook for you. My place.

A long pause. Then—

MAYA:

Are you sure? That feels like crossing another line.

DECLAN:

We crossed all the lines last night. Besides, I make a decent pasta, and you've been feeding me Highland's community meals for weeks. It's my turn.

MAYA:

What do you mean?

DECLAN:

I mean dinner. Just dinner. You've shown me your world—let me show you mine. 7 PM?

MAYA:

Okay. Should I bring anything?

DECLAN:

Just yourself. And an appetite for mediocre cooking.

MAYA:

I doubt it's mediocre.

DECLAN:

We'll find out together.

My phone sits silent on the desk, our dinner plans confirmed. I should go back to reviewing Highland's financial projections, preparing talking points for Monday's board meeting. But something about tonight feels important—not as a test or revelation, but as a chance to spend time with Maya away from Highland's intensity and Pierce Enterprises' pressure.

For once, I want to just be Declan cooking dinner for someone I care about, instead of CEO Declan Pierce calculating corporate strategy.

Because maybe that's who I really am underneath all the rest.

13

Maya

"Turn around," Lianne says from her perch on my bed, surrounded by three different dresses she brought over like this is some kind of fashion emergency. "I need to see how that one looks from the back."

I spin in front of my bedroom mirror, studying the way the navy-blue dress falls just above my knees. It's borrowed from Lianne's closet—something she calls "casual but elevated"—though it probably cost more than my monthly grocery budget.

"You guys really are serious about this, aren't you?" Lianne's voice carries a note I can't quite identify. Not disapproval, exactly, but something close to concern.

"Serious about what?" I smooth the dress over my hips, trying to decide if it's too much for dinner at someone's house. Even someone's very expensive house in the Hollywood Hills.

"About each other. About whatever this thing is between you and Declan." Lianne stands and walks over to adjust the dress's neckline. "Maya, when's the last time you cared this much about what you wore to dinner?"

She's right, and we both know it. I can't remember the last time I spent twenty minutes staring into my closet, or called my best friend for wardrobe assistance, or felt butterflies in my stomach about seeing someone I've already spent the night with.

"It's just dinner," I say, though the words sound unconvincing even to me.

"Just dinner at his house. His very impressive, very expensive house." Lianne meets my eyes in the mirror. "Maya, I need to tell you something about men like Declan."

Something in her tone makes me turn away from my reflection. "Men like Declan?"

"Wealthy, powerful, from established families." Lianne settles back onto my bed, her usual humor replaced by something more serious. "Remember Cameron?"

"Of course." I sit beside her, the navy dress suddenly feeling too formal. They dated for about a year, but I only met him twice, and just when I thought things were serious between them, they were done. "But you never told me the details."

"Cameron Phillip Arthur Judd. Old money, Pacific Palisades family, everything I thought I wanted." Lianne's voice grows quiet, distant. "We met when I was planning his sister's wedding, remember? He was charming, successful, said all the right things about supporting my career and loving how independent I was."

"What happened?"

"His mother happened. His board of directors happened. His trust fund that came with strings happened." Lianne meets my eyes, and I see old hurt there, carefully controlled but never fully healed. "He loved me, Maya. I believe that. But when push came to shove, when his family made it clear that a working-class event planner wasn't suitable for a Judd, someone whose foster parents cleaned houses and worked construction, he chose their approval over us."

Now I understand why Lianne always gets that look when Cameron's name comes up, why she's been so protective about my relationship with Declan.

"I'm sorry, Lianne. I had no idea it was that bad."

"Ancient history," she says, but her smile doesn't quite reach her eyes. She stands and smooths down my dress, back to practical mode. "Just promise me you'll keep your guard up tonight, okay? I don't want to see you get hurt the way I did."

"I promise."

She gathers the other dresses, preparing to leave me to finish getting ready. At my bedroom door, she pauses. "For what it's worth, I think he cares about you. I've seen the way he looks at you and believe me, I want a man to look at me just like that." She chuckles then turns serious. "I just want to make sure he cares enough to choose you when it matters."

Declan's house in the Hollywood Hills is nothing like what I expected. Instead of the cold, modernist mansion I imagined, it's a 1940s Spanish Colonial with warm stucco walls, arched doorways, and a courtyard garden that feels more like a retreat than a display of wealth.

"This is beautiful," I say as he leads me through the front

door into a living room with exposed beam ceilings and windows that overlook the twinkling lights of LA below. But as I take in the details—the original artwork on the walls, the quality of the furnishings, the way everything seems carefully curated yet effortless—the reality of our different worlds becomes impossible to ignore.

"It was my grandfather's," Declan says, setting his keys on a console table that looks like it's been in the family for decades. "He bought it in the 1950s when this area was still orange groves and Hollywood dreams. My father always wanted to tear it down and build something more impressive, but I could never bring myself to change it."

I walk to the windows, taking in the view of the city spreading out below us. From here, downtown LA is a cluster of lights in the distance, Highland Community Center invisible but somehow still present in my thoughts. This view—this perspective of looking down on the city—feels symbolic in a way that makes me uncomfortable.

"Maya." Declan's voice is soft behind me, and when I turn, I catch something in his expression. Not quite worry, but a tension that wasn't there during our drive up the winding hillside roads. "Are you having second thoughts?"

The question feels loaded, as if he's asking about more than just being here tonight. "No second thoughts," I tell him honestly. "Just... taking it all in. This house, this evening, the fact that I'm here with you instead of working on those financial reports that are due Monday."

"We could go back to Highland if you'd prefer. Or I could take you home. We don't have to—"

I close the distance between us, placing my hand on his chest to stop his worried rambling. His heart is beating faster than it should be for someone who's simply hosting dinner. "Declan, I want to be here. With you. I want to see what happens when we stop being Maya Navarro, the community organizer and Declan Pierce, the CEO, and just be... us. Even if it's just for tonight."

The words slip out before I can stop them, revealing the uncertainty I've been trying to push down all day.

Relief flickers across his features. "Good. Because I've been thinking about getting you alone like this since we danced at the festival."

"Just since the festival?"

"Since you scattered those petition papers across my office floor and looked at me like I was a problem you intended to solve." His smile is soft, intimate, but it doesn't quite reach his eyes. "You were magnificent when you were angry."

"I was terrified when I was angry. I'd never confronted anyone like you before."

"Like me?"

"Completely out of my league." I gesture around his living room, at the inherited wealth and casual luxury that surrounds us.

Declan's hands settle at my waist, pulling me closer. "Maya, you were never out of my league. If anything, it's the reverse. You're fighting for something that matters, something bigger than yourself. You have passion and conviction and the kind of courage that makes people follow you into impossible battles."

"And you have the power to save or destroy everything I care about."

"No." His voice is firm, almost urgent. "I have the power

to advocate for Highland within Pierce Enterprises' structure. But you have the power to save Highland through your research, your presentation, your refusal to give up even when the odds are impossible."

I study his face, noting the genuine conviction in his expression, but also the way his jaw tightens when he mentions Pierce Enterprises. "You really believe that?"

"I really believe that Highland's future depends more on your determination than on my corporate influence." He lifts his hand to trace my cheek with his fingertips, and the gesture feels almost desperate. "Which is why whatever happens in Monday's board meeting, whatever decisions get made about preservation or demolition, tonight is just about us."

"Just about us," I repeat, testing how the words feel. But Monday feels closer than it did this morning, more real, more threatening.

"Just about us." Declan leans down to brush a soft kiss across my lips. "Would you like some wine? I have a bottle of 1982 Chateau Le Pin that's been waiting for a special occasion."

"I'm going to pretend I know what that means and nod, impressed," I say, tilting my head. "Is this a special occasion?"

"The first evening I've spent with Maya Navarro instead of Highland Community Center's executive director? Definitely a special occasion."

While Declan opens wine in the kitchen, I explore his living room, noting the mix of inherited family pieces and carefully chosen modern additions. Books line built-in shelves—not just business texts but fiction, poetry, volumes on public policy and urban planning. A guitar sits in one corner, well-used rather than decorative. It's a room that tells the story of three generations, of wealth accumulated and preserved, of legacy passed down through family lines.

The contrast with our folding chairs and borrowed space and constant fundraising is stark, a reminder that we come from such different worlds. In his world, problems get solved with phone calls and checkbooks rather than bake sales and community meetings.

"You play?" I ask when he returns with two glasses of wine.

"Badly. But it helps me think." He hands me a glass, his fingers brushing mine in a contact that sends warmth spiraling up my arm. "My grandfather taught me when I was twelve. He said music was important for men in business, that it kept them human."

"Smart grandfather."

"He would have liked you. He believed in community investment, supporting local organizations. He used to say that a man's worth wasn't measured by what he accumulated but by what he contributed."

"That sounds like our philosophy."

"Maybe that's why I was drawn to your approach from the beginning." Declan settles onto the sofa, and I join him, noting how the expensive cushions bring us closer together. "My father never understood his father's community focus. He thought it was inefficient, sentimental."

"What do you think?"

"I think my grandfather understood something about building lasting value that my father missed." Declan takes a sip of wine, his gaze thoughtful, but I catch the way his fingers tighten around the glass. "Highland has been serving the community for twenty years with minimal resources. Pierce Enterprises builds luxury developments that generate profit for five years and then get sold off. Which approach creates more lasting value?"

"You're asking the wrong person. I'm obviously biased toward my father's model."

"You're exactly the right person to ask." Declan sets down his wine and turns to face me more directly, and there's an intensity in his expression that makes my pulse quicken. "Maya, I need you to understand something. The collaboration with Highland, the research into historic preservation, the advocacy I'm planning for Monday's meeting—none of that is about impressing you or winning your approval."

"What is it about?"

"It's about discovering that there are better ways to measure success than the approach my father taught me. It's about learning that some things are worth preserving even when demolition would be more profitable."

I study his face, searching for any hint of corporate calculation or strategic positioning. Instead, I see vulnerability, uncertainty, a man questioning everything he was raised to believe about business and success. But underneath that, there's something else—a tension that suggests he's fighting battles I don't fully understand.

"Declan." I set down my own wine and move closer, close enough to see the gold flecks in his gray eyes, close enough to notice the faint lines of stress around them. "Can I tell you something?"

"Anything."

"When you first proposed the collaboration, I thought it

was an elaborate stalling tactic. A way to neutralize Highland's opposition while you finalized demolition plans."

"And now?"

"Now I think you're a man who's trying to figure out who he wants to be when he's not living up to his father's expectations." I reach up to trace the line of his jaw with my fingertips, feeling the tension there. "The difference is that my father's legacy aligns with who I want to be. Yours doesn't."

"No," he agrees quietly, and for a moment, his carefully controlled expression cracks, revealing something that looks like fear. "It doesn't."

"So what do you want, Declan? If you could build anything, be anyone, what would that look like?"

He's quiet for a moment, his gaze drifting toward the windows where LA's lights twinkle in the darkness. When he speaks, his voice is barely above a whisper. "I want to build things that matter. Developments that strengthen communities instead of displacing them. Projects that create value for residents, not just investors."

"That sounds like a worthy goal."

"It sounds impossible within Pierce Enterprises' current structure." His phone buzzes on the side table—probably work emails he's ignoring for tonight—and the sound seems to pull him back from wherever his thoughts had wandered.

"Maybe Pierce Enterprises' structure needs to change."

"Maybe it does." Declan's gaze returns to my face, and I see him make a visible effort to push away whatever was troubling him. "But enough about corporate philosophy. I didn't bring you here to discuss business strategy."

"What did you bring me here for?"

"To show you who I am when I'm not representing Pierce

Enterprises. To find out who you are when you're not fighting for Highland's survival." His hand slides up to cup my face, and there's an urgency in the gesture that makes me wonder if he's thinking about how little time we might have. "To explore this thing between us without professional obligations getting in the way."

"And what is this thing between us?"

"I don't know yet. But I'd like to find out."

He leans down to kiss me, and this time there's nothing tentative about it. This kiss is hungry, searching, full of the desire that's been building between us for weeks. But underneath the passion, I sense something else—a desperation that suggests he needs this connection as much as I do, maybe more.

When I respond, parting my lips under his, he makes a soft sound of approval that sends heat pooling low in my stomach.

"Maya." My name comes out rough when we break apart, and there's something in his voice—not just desire, but an urgency that makes me wonder if he's thinking about Monday too. About how this might be our last night before everything changes.

"No more talking," I whisper. "Just show me."

Declan's response is to deepen our kiss, his hands sliding down to my waist and then lower, pulling me closer until I'm practically in his lap. I can feel the solid warmth of his chest against mine, can catch the scent of his cologne mixed with wine and something that's purely him.

When he trails kisses down my neck, finding the sensitive spot where my pulse flutters, I arch against him, wanting more contact, more pressure, more everything.

"You're beautiful," he murmurs against my throat. "Do you know how hard it's been to maintain professional boundaries when all I wanted was to touch you like this?"

"Show me how hard it's been," I breathe, and I feel him smile against my skin.

"With pleasure."

He lifts me easily, carrying me toward what I assume is his bedroom, and I'm struck by how natural this feels despite the surreal setting. Not rushed or desperate, but inevitable.

Declan's bedroom continues the house's warm, comfortable aesthetic—a king-sized bed with soft linens, windows that overlook the garden, art that feels personal rather than decorative. It's a room designed for rest and intimacy, not for impressing visitors, but the quality of everything reminds me again of the gulf between our worlds.

He sets me down beside the bed and steps back slightly, his gaze traveling over my face with something that looks like wonder mixed with something I can't quite identify.

"What?" I ask, suddenly self-conscious.

"I just want to remember this moment. The way you look right now, the way the moonlight catches your hair, the fact that you're here with me." There's an intensity in his voice that suggests he's memorizing more than just this moment—as if he's preparing for the possibility that there might not be many more.

"I'm here," I confirm, reaching for the buttons of his shirt. "And I'm not going anywhere."

"Maya." He catches my hands, stilling my movements, and for a second, I see something like regret flash across his features. "We don't have to rush this. We have all night."

All night. As if that's all we have.

"I don't want to rush it," I whisper.

In response, he releases my hands and allows me to continue unbuttoning his shirt. When I push the fabric off his shoulders, revealing the broad chest and defined muscles I've been imagining, I take a moment to simply appreciate the view.

"Your turn," he says softly, his hands moving to the zipper at the back of my dress.

The reveal feels familiar now, but no less electric. When my dress pools at my feet and Declan's gaze travels over my body, I remember how he looked at me in my small apartment—but this time, there's an added intimacy of knowing exactly how his hands will feel on my skin.

"Perfect," he murmurs, drawing me back into his arms. "Absolutely perfect."

The feeling of skin against skin is electric. Every point of contact sends warmth shooting through my nervous system, and when Declan's hands begin to explore—tracing the curve of my waist, the line of my spine, the sensitive skin at my hip— I realize I've never felt so completely present in my own body.

I sigh into his touch, my body responding with a hunger that's been building for weeks. His hands are gentle but confident, mapping my curves with reverent attention that makes me feel both cherished and desired. When he unclasps my bra, letting it join my dress on the floor, I don't feel exposed—I feel seen.

"You're so beautiful," he growls, his voice low and rough, like gravel dragged over silk as he lowers me onto the bed. His breath is hot against my skin, and I shiver as his lips find my nipple, sucking it into his mouth with a slow, deliberate pull that makes my back archd. His tongue flicks over the sensitive peak, teasing it into a hard little bud, and I can't help but moan, the sound clawing its way out of my throat. His hand is on my other breast, fingers pinching and rolling the nipple with just the right amount of pressure, sending jolts of electricity straight to my core.

My body is on fire, every nerve ending alive with want. I gasp as he moves lower, trailing kisses down my stomach and lower still until he settles between my thighs, parting my legs with gentle hands. My pulse hammers in my throat as he looks up at me, eyes dark with hunger, seeking permission. I nod, unable to find words, and then his mouth is on me, hot and insistent.

"Oh God," I breathe, my fingers tangling in his hair, anchoring myself to him as pleasure spirals through me. His tongue is relentless, circling and flicking with devastating precision. My hips rise off the bed, seeking more of this exquisite torture.

Through half-closed eyes, I watch him watching me, and there's something in his gaze—a fierce concentration, a need to memorize every response, every gasp. As if he's cataloging what makes me fall apart. When he slides one finger inside me, then two, curling them forward while his tongue continues its assault, the pressure building inside me threatens to shatter me completely.

"Declan," I gasp, teetering on the edge of something monumental. My thighs begin to tremble as he increases his pace, his fingers working in perfect rhythm with his mouth. "I'm going to—"

"Let go," he murmurs against me, the vibration of his

voice sending new sensations rippling through my body. "I want to watch you come apart."

When the wave finally breaks, it's unlike anything I've experienced before—not just physical release but something that feels like surrender. I cry out his name as pleasure pulses through me, my body arching and tensing, then melting into the luxurious sheets beneath me.

Before I can fully recover, Declan is moving up my body, his lips capturing mine in a kiss that tastes of me and him together. I can feel him hard against my thigh, his control slipping as he rocks against me with obvious need. My hands slide down his chest, feeling the rapid beat of his heart before continuing lower to wrap around him. He hisses in a breath at my touch, his eyes fluttering closed for a moment.

"Maya," he whispers, his voice strained. "I need—"

"I know what you need," I murmur, guiding him toward me. "I need it too."

He reaches toward the nightstand, fumbling for a moment before producing a condom. I watch as he tears the packet open with his teeth, the small action somehow intensely erotic. When he positions himself above me again, there's a vulnerability in his expression that catches me off guard.

"Are you sure?" he asks, brushing a strand of hair from my face with gentle fingers.

In answer, I wrap my legs around his hips and pull him closer. Our eyes lock as he enters me slowly—inch by deliberate inch—the stretch and fullness making me gasp. He pauses, giving me time to adjust, his forehead pressed against mine as we share the same breath, the same heartbeat. When he begins to move, it's with a restraint that speaks of both consideration and barely leashed desire.

"You feel incredible," he whispers against my ear, his voice strained with the effort of maintaining control. "So perfect around me."

I tighten my legs around him, urging him deeper, wanting more of this connection that feels both new and somehow inevitable. My hands explore the muscles of his back, feeling them flex and tense with each controlled thrust. There's something almost reverent in the way he's moving within me, as if he's savoring every sensation, memorizing every response.

"More," I breathe, nails digging into his shoulders. "I need more of you."

His rhythm changes at my urging, thrusts becoming deeper, more insistent. The careful restraint he's maintained begins to crack as his breathing grows ragged against my neck. I arch to meet each movement, feeling the tension building inside me again, different this time but no less powerful.

"Look at me," he commands softly, and when I open my eyes, the intensity of his gaze nearly undoes me. There's something raw and unguarded in his expression that makes my chest tighten with an emotion I'm not ready to name.

Our bodies move together with increasing urgency, the room filled with the sounds of our pleasure—soft moans, whispered encouragements, skin against skin. When he shifts his angle slightly, hitting a spot inside me that sends sparks shooting behind my eyelids, I cry out, my body clenching around him.

"That's it," he murmurs, one hand sliding between us to

circle my most sensitive spot. "Come for me again, Maya. I want to feel you."

His words and touch push me over the edge, and I'm falling, drowning in sensation as pleasure crashes through me in waves. This time, he follows me over, his rhythm faltering as he buries his face against my neck with a deep groan that vibrates through my entire body. I feel him pulsing inside me, his arms trembling slightly as he holds himself above me, careful not to crush me with his weight.

For several minutes, we stay like this, connected and breathless, his heartbeat thundering against my chest. When he finally pulls away to dispose of the condom, the loss of contact leaves me feeling strangely bereft. But he returns quickly, gathering me against his side, his fingers tracing lazy patterns on my skin.

"We're really in trouble, aren't we?" I trail off, unable to articulate the tangled emotions welling up inside me. The weight of Monday's meeting looms larger now, a shadow stretching across this perfect moment.

"Probably," he agrees, his voice soft in the dim light of his bedroom. He pulls me closer, pressing a kiss to my temple that feels like both a promise and an apology. "But right now, in this moment, I don't care."

I rest my head on his chest, listening to his heartbeat gradually slow as the city continues its own rhythm outside his windows. "I don't either."

Declan

THE CONFERENCE ROOM feels different at 10 AM on a Monday morning, though I can't quite put my finger on why. I'm sitting at the same mahogany table where Highland's initial fate was discussed months ago, but this time Maya is beside me, her presentation materials spread across the polished surface like battle plans.

She's wearing a professional navy dress that brings out her eyes, her hair pulled back in a style that's both polished and approachable. Her hands are steady as she connects her laptop to the projection system, but I catch the slight tremor in her fingers that betrays her nerves.

"Ready?" I ask quietly.

"Ready," she replies, though her voice carries the weight of everything Highland's community is counting on.

The board members file in—Harrison, Patricia, Donovan, Melanie, and Roderick—all carrying tablets and wearing the kind of neutral expressions that reveal nothing about their intentions. But I notice Harrison's slight frown when he sees the extent of Maya's preparation, the comprehensive materials that suggest this isn't just a community wish list.

"Miss Navarro," Harrison settles at the head of the table. "Thank you for joining us this morning. We're looking forward to your presentation."

"Thank you for the opportunity." Maya moves to the front of the room with the same determined energy she brought to my office six weeks ago. "I'm excited to share Highland Community Center's vision for historic preservation and community-business partnership."

For the next forty-five minutes, Maya delivers a presentation that's masterful—clear, comprehensive, and compelling. She walks through Highland's twenty-year history, demonstrates the community impact of their programs, and presents detailed financial projections for mixed-use development that incorporates historic preservation.

The numbers are impressive. Transit-oriented development incentives, historic tax credits, and premium pricing for authentic neighborhood character combine to make preservation potentially more profitable than demolition. Maya answers technical questions with confidence, addresses concerns about construction costs with realistic estimates, and demonstrates that Highland's preservation could be both good business and good citizenship.

I watch the board members' faces as she speaks, noting Patricia's obvious interest and Donovan's thoughtful questions. Even Melanie seems engaged by the financial projections. For the first time since this collaboration began, I feel genuine hope that we might actually win this.

When Maya finishes, the conference room is quiet. The

board members review her materials, occasionally murmuring to each other, while Maya returns to her seat beside me. I catch her hand under the table, squeezing gently in what I hope feels like encouragement.

"Thank you, Miss Navarro," Harrison says finally. "This is a comprehensive proposal. Before we proceed to deliberation, I have an update that affects our timeline considerations."

Maya nods, her professional composure intact despite what I know must be racing anxiety.

"The Metro expansion utility conflicts have been resolved ahead of schedule," Harrison continues, pulling out his tablet. "The transit hub will open as originally planned, which significantly impacts our development strategy."

I feel Maya tense beside me as she processes this information. We'd built part of our argument around the delays creating opportunities for Pierce Enterprises to position itself advantageously.

"This is excellent news for the Anderson Project's market positioning," Harrison continues. "It also means we can proceed with luxury development on our original aggressive timeline without the infrastructure complications that were affecting investor confidence."

"How does this impact Highland's proposal?" Maya asks, her voice steady despite the obvious blow to one of her key arguments.

"It changes the fundamental equation we're evaluating," Harrison replies. "With Metro complications resolved, luxury condos become significantly more profitable than mixed-use development with preservation requirements."

The temperature in the room seems to drop. I can feel

Maya's growing realization that external circumstances have undermined her carefully constructed proposal through no fault of her own.

"However," I interject, "Highland's proposal still offers superior long-term value. Historic preservation provides permanent tax benefits, community partnerships create sustained positive PR value, and authentic neighborhood character commands premium pricing for decades rather than quarters."

"Valid points," Donovan acknowledges. "But we have fiduciary responsibilities to maximize shareholder return."

"Which Highland's proposal does," Maya says firmly. "The financial projections demonstrate twelve percent higher profit margins over ten years compared to conventional luxury development."

"Projected margins," Melanie corrects. "Mixed-use development involves regulatory uncertainties that could impact those projections significantly."

I can see Maya's frustration building, but she maintains her professional demeanor. "All development involves regulatory risk. Historic preservation actually provides more regulatory certainty through established tax credit programs."

"Miss Navarro raises excellent points," Patricia says. "I'm impressed by the thoroughness of this proposal."

"As am I," Donovan adds. "The community partnership model could position Pierce Enterprises as an industry leader."

Harrison's expression grows more serious. "While I appreciate the community engagement this process represents, I have concerns about the complexity Miss Navarro is proposing. Mixed-use development requires extensive coordination with community organizations that may not share our timeline priorities. Historic preservation involves regulatory reviews that could delay construction significantly."

"Delays that are offset by substantial financial benefits," I argue. "The tax incentives alone justify the additional coordination costs."

"Perhaps. But Pierce Enterprises has built its reputation on reliable project delivery and predictable returns." Harrison leans forward. "This proposal, while innovative, represents a fundamental departure from our proven development model."

I feel the momentum shifting against us, see Maya's growing realization that her brilliant proposal is being dismissed not on its merits but on Pierce Enterprises' institutional conservatism.

"I'd like to call for a formal vote," I say, surprising everyone including myself. "Highland's preservation proposal versus luxury condo development."

Harrison looks genuinely startled. "Declan, I'm not sure a formal vote is necessary. We could continue deliberating—"

"I think it's essential," I interrupt, standing up. "This decision will define Pierce Enterprises' approach to community development for years to come. The board should go on record about whether we prioritize community partnership or default to maximum short-term profits."

Maya looks at me with something that might be admiration or concern. Around the table, board members exchange uncomfortable glances.

"The community has presented a proposal that offers

superior long-term returns while strengthening Pierce Enterprises' reputation and positioning us as industry leaders in sustainable development," I continue, my voice growing more passionate. "If we reject that in favor of conventional luxury condos, we're choosing the easy path over the innovative one."

"Declan," Harrison's voice carries a warning. "You're advocating very strongly for a proposal that aligns with your personal feelings about this situation."

"I'm advocating for a proposal that makes good business sense while honoring the community partnerships we've been building for months." I look directly at him. "If Pierce Enterprises can't recognize superior value when it's presented with comprehensive research and compelling financials, then we need to question our decision-making process."

The tension in the room is electric. Maya sits perfectly still beside me, but I can feel her shock at my public challenge to Harrison's authority.

"Very well," Harrison says finally, his voice cold. "All in favor of proceeding with luxury condos as originally planned?"

Melanie raises her hand immediately. Roderick follows after a moment's hesitation. Harrison pauses, clearly aware that his vote will be scrutinized, then raises his own hand.

Three votes for demolition.

"All in favor of mixed-use development with Highland preservation?"

I raise my hand without hesitation. Patricia joins me, followed by Donovan who looks genuinely conflicted but ultimately votes for preservation.

Three to three.

The silence that follows feels eternal.

"Three to three," Harrison announces. "In the case of tied board votes, Pierce Enterprises bylaws require the chairman to cast the deciding vote."

My heart pounds as I realize Highland's fate comes down to Harrison's single decision. The man who's spent months trying to minimize community input is now the sole arbiter of Highland's future.

Harrison looks around the table, his gaze lingering on Maya's expectant face, then on mine. "Given our fiduciary responsibility to maximize shareholder return, and considering the increased profitability of luxury development with resolved Metro complications…"

He pauses, and I can see Maya holding her breath.

"I vote for proceeding with luxury condos as originally planned."

Four to three. Highland loses by Harrison's single vote.

The silence that follows is deafening. I watch Maya's face as the reality sinks in—months of work, brilliant research, community hopes, all dismissed by one man's decision to prioritize profit margins over partnership.

"Motion carries," Harrison says with obvious satisfaction. "Pierce Enterprises will proceed with demolition and luxury condo construction to begin in six weeks. Miss Navarro, we appreciate your thorough presentation, but the board has decided to maintain our original development strategy."

Maya sits perfectly still for a moment, her face carefully blank. Then she stands with mechanical precision and begins gathering her materials.

"Miss Navarro," Harrison calls after her. "Pierce Enterprises will provide generous relocation assistance to ease Highland's transition."

Maya pauses, her back still turned to the table. When she speaks, her voice is steady but carrying an edge that makes everyone pay attention.

"Keep your assistance, Mr. Gordon." She turns to face the board, and there's something in her expression—not defeat, but a cold fury that's more intimidating than any emotional outburst. "Highland Community Center has served this community for twenty years with minimal resources and maximum impact. We've survived economic downturns, natural disasters, and systematic neglect by city officials who forgot we existed."

She steps closer to the table, her presence suddenly commanding the room.

"We'll survive Pierce Enterprises too. But I want this board to understand something." Her gaze moves from Harrison to each board member in turn. "You didn't just vote against preserving a building. You voted against twenty years of after-school programs that kept children safe while their parents worked multiple jobs. You voted against ESL classes that helped immigrants become citizens. You voted against cultural preservation that maintained connections between generations."

Her voice grows stronger, more passionate.

"You voted against emergency shelter during crises, job training for teenagers aging out of foster care, and citizenship test preparation for people pursuing the American dream. You voted against community meetings where neighbors solved problems together instead of calling police. You voted against the kind of social infrastructure that actually prevents the urban decay your luxury developments claim to solve."

The board members shift uncomfortably, but Maya isn't finished.

"Most importantly, you voted to prove that when corporations promise community partnership, they mean partnership that doesn't cost them anything. You've demonstrated that Pierce Enterprises considers community engagement a marketing strategy, not a business principle."

She gathers the last of her materials, her movements deliberate and controlled.

"Highland will relocate. We'll rebuild our programs in multiple locations, probably serving families more effectively than centralized programming ever could. We'll prove that community strength doesn't depend on corporate generosity or the buildings that house it." Maya's smile is sharp, determined. "And when we do, Pierce Enterprises will be remembered as the company that chose profit over partnership when given the opportunity to build something meaningful."

She heads toward the door, then pauses to look back at the board.

"Thank you for the education about how corporate democracy actually works. Highland's families will benefit from understanding exactly what they're up against."

The door closes behind her with a soft click, leaving the board members sitting in uncomfortable silence.

"Well," Harrison says finally, clearing his throat. "I think that went as well as could be expected. Declan, I'll need you to coordinate the transition timeline with our construction team."

I stare at him, processing what he's asking. Coordinate Highland's destruction. Manage the demolition of everything Maya cares about after watching her deliver the most powerful defense of community values I've ever witnessed.

"Of course," I hear myself say. "I'll handle the details."

But as the board members file out, discussing construction schedules and profit projections like they didn't just witness Maya Navarro systematically dismantle their justifications for corporate callousness, I know that I can't handle this.

I can't be part of Highland's destruction after watching Maya fight with such fierce intelligence and moral clarity.

Not when she just proved that some things are worth defending even when the defense is doomed to fail.

Not when I've seen what courage actually looks like when it refuses to accept defeat gracefully.

15

Maya

Four to three.

That's all it took to destroy everything my father built, everything I've fought to preserve, everything these families depend on.

Four hands raised for demolition. Three for preservation. Highland Community Center condemned by Harrison Gordon's single deciding vote after a tied board—so close I can still taste the possibility of victory that slipped away when he chose profit over partnership.

And then there's the folder.

The parking structure swallows the sound of my heels against the concrete, and I'm three levels down, digging through my bag for keys I can't seem to find when I hear Declan call my name.

I don't turn around. I've done enough turning around for Declan Pierce.

"Maya. Please."

It's the *please* that stops me, because in all the weeks I've known him I've never once heard him use the word, and there's a part of me—the part that lay against his chest two nights ago and believed every quiet thing he told me about his mother and his father and the man he was trying to become—that still wants it to mean something.

I turn around.

He's loosened his tie somewhere between the boardroom and here, and he looks like a man who's been running, which I suppose he has been, and for half a breath the sight of him reaches something in me I thought I'd closed off, before I remember exactly what Harrison pressed into my hands on my way to the elevator.

"I'm going to find another way," he says, closing the distance between us. "The vote isn't the end of this. I have alternative proposals, investors I can approach, ways to—"

"Stop." The word comes out flat, and he does.

I pull the folder from my bag and hold it up between us, and I watch the recognition move across his face as he takes in the Pierce Enterprises letterhead and understands, before I say a single word, exactly what I'm holding.

"Do you know what this is?"

He doesn't answer, which is its own kind of answer.

"The minutes from your board meeting. The first one—the morning after my protest, when you sat down and decided how you were going to handle me." I open the folder, though I don't need to; I've read it enough times in the last twenty minutes that the words are burned behind my eyes.

"I want us to control the narrative. Right now Maya Navarro is writing the story, and we're cast as the villains. If we bring her to the table, we become partners seeking solutions."

I look up. He hasn't moved.

"There's a line I keep coming back to," I say, and I hold my voice level, because the only other option is screaming, and I refuse to hand him my screaming in a parking garage. *"Alternatives we'll help her discover don't exist. By the end of the process, Highland will have exhausted every option, and Pierce Enterprises will be positioned as having gone above and beyond."*

I close the folder.

"You said that. In a room full of people, the day before you reached across my father's desk and called us partners."

"You're not wrong," he says, and the quiet in his voice is almost worse than a denial would have been.

"That's all you have? *You're not wrong?*"

"What would you like me to say, Maya—that I didn't sit in that room and pitch your community as a problem to be managed?" He doesn't look away, and I hate that he doesn't, because it would be so much easier if he were a man who couldn't hold my eyes. "Every word in that folder is mine. I meant all of it when I said it."

"And then?" Because there's an *and then*; I can hear it waiting behind his teeth.

He's quiet a moment. "And then I spent six weeks inside the place I'd planned to tear down. I watched you teach a roomful of teenagers a dance I couldn't pronounce. I ate Rosa's siopao standing up in your kitchen because there was nowhere to sit." His jaw tightens. "I can't give you the day it stopped being a strategy, Maya. I only know that it did. And I know exactly how that sounds."

And there it is—the thing that's been clawing at me since I unfolded these pages outside the conference room while my whole body still believed we'd lost that vote together, as equals, as two people standing on the same side of something.

"That's the problem, Declan." My voice holds, and I'm proud of it the way Papa would have been proud of it. "You can't tell me when it stopped being a strategy. And if *you* can't tell, how am I ever supposed to? Every soft thing you said to me, every time you let me keep believing Highland had a chance—I have to hold all of it up against this folder now and guess which version was the real one." I press the folder against his chest, and he takes it, because what else is he going to do with his hands. "You've made it so I can never know. You've turned every good memory into a question I don't get to answer."

"Maya." Just my name, said the way he said it that first afternoon in his office, the way that used to send those traitorous flutters straight through me. "I never wanted—"

"I believe that." And I do, which is somehow the cruelest part of it. "I believe you never wanted this. But wanting and doing were never the same thing for your father, and I'm only now understanding they aren't the same thing for you either."

I leave him standing between a concrete pillar and a row of cars worth more than Highland's roof, the folder in his hands, and I don't let myself come apart until I'm sealed inside my own car with the doors locked and the engine cold.

Thirty seconds. The same thirty seconds I allowed myself in his elevator six weeks ago—and then I dry my face and wrap my hands around the wheel, because crying never saved a single thing my father built, and it isn't going to save Highland now.

. . .

The drive back to Highland passes in a blur of downtown traffic and a fury gone cold and quiet—not the heat I carried out of that boardroom, but the patient, calculated anger that comes from watching intelligent people make morally bankrupt decisions while congratulating themselves on their fiduciary responsibility, and from finally understanding that I was a line item on someone's strategy long before I was ever anyone's partner.

I park outside Highland and sit for a moment, staring at the building that's been sentenced to death. In six weeks, bulldozers will tear down these walls. In six weeks, twenty years of community history will become rubble so Pierce Enterprises can build luxury condos for people who will never understand what this place meant.

I force myself out of the car and through Highland's front doors, into the main hall where our community gathered this morning with such hope. Around me lie the scattered remains of what was supposed to be a celebration—coffee cups and the pastries Rosa brought for the good news we were so sure was coming, the banners the teenagers painted reading *Highland Forever*, the flowers from Mrs. Hidalgo's garden meant to mark a victory. All of it looks like decoration for a funeral now.

"Maya?" Rosa's voice cuts through the quiet. She stands in the kitchen doorway with a dish towel in her hands and her face still bright with hope. "Any word from Pierce Enterprises?"

I look around the hall at the dozen community members still here, waiting—Tita Sol organizing tomorrow's after-school schedules, Carlo crouched over a computer for the evening ESL class, families who've made Highland their second home for decades, all of them trusting me to save what none of us can bear to lose.

"Pierce Enterprises voted for demolition." The words come out flat, emptied of everything. "Highland is going to be torn down."

The silence that follows is the worst sound I've ever heard. Rosa lowers her dish towel. Tita Sol stops mid-motion over her papers. Carlo looks up from the keyboard, his young face working through what this means for the only place that has ever felt like his.

"But your presentation," Tita Sol says slowly. "The research, the projections—surely they understood—"

"They understood. They just didn't care." I cross to the windows that look out toward downtown, toward the tower where six people in good suits decided we weren't worth the trouble.

"And Declan?" Lianne asks, very quietly. "What about the collaboration?"

What about Declan. What about the man who spent six weeks letting me believe the collaboration meant something it had never, on paper, been allowed to mean.

"Declan voted with us," I say, because it's true, and because the truth is the only thing I have left to give them. "But it wasn't enough. And the rest of it—" I stop. *The rest of it is mine to carry, not theirs.* "The rest of it doesn't matter now."

My phone buzzes against my hip. I don't have to look to know it's him; he's been at it since the parking garage, the screen lighting again and again on the drive over.

DECLAN:

Maya, please. Let me explain. I know how
the folder reads. I know what it looks like.
Give me ten minutes.

I turn the phone face-down on the windowsill.

"Maya." Tito Ricky comes out of my office, his expression grave; Lianne must have called him. "I'm so sorry. Tell me what you need."

"Our legal options. All of them."

"Limited," he admits, lowering himself into a folding chair, looking older than his sixty-five years. "Pierce Enterprises owns the property, holds every permit, and followed proper notification procedures. We can file challenges on environmental impact or historic significance, but those buy delay, not survival. Six months. A year, if we're lucky and very strategic."

"Then we buy the year, and we use it to find something they can't take from us with a vote." I hear my own voice harden into something I don't quite recognize. "I'm done depending on Pierce Enterprises to do the decent thing. Highland's future can't sit in the hands of people who get to change their minds about whether we deserve to exist."

Tito Ricky studies me for a long moment. "That's a different fight than the one we've been having."

"It's the only one worth having anymore."

He goes off to make calls, and Rosa appears at my side with a cup of coffee I didn't ask for and the steady, unhurried attention of a woman who raised four children, buried a husband, and has never once been fooled by my armor.

"You told them about the vote," she says. "You didn't tell them about whatever else happened today."

I wrap both hands around the coffee. "There's nothing else to tell."

"Anak." She says it gently, and then she waits, and she lets the silence do what silence does.

"I found out the collaboration was never real," I say at last, and the words cost more than I expect them to. "Not at the start. They planned it as a way to manage me—to keep me quiet and looking reasonable while they ran out the clock. I have it in writing, Rosa. His words, on the page."

Rosa is quiet for a while, and when she finally speaks she doesn't reach for the thing I'm braced against. She doesn't tell me he's a good man, doesn't tell me to give him the benefit of the doubt, doesn't tell me the way he looked at me must have meant something. She knows better than to argue a woman out of a wound while it's still open.

"Then you have every right to your anger," she says. "Don't let anyone rush you out of it, including me."

I look at her, surprised, and feel my throat close.

"But I'll say one thing, and then I'll leave it alone." She covers my hand on the cup with her own. "People are not one thing, anak. Your father was the gentlest man I ever knew, and I once watched him throw a city inspector out that front door by his collar. I have known saints who lied, and liars who showed up when it mattered most." She squeezes my hand. "I'm not telling you what that man is. I'm telling you that a folder doesn't get to be the whole answer, any more than a kiss did. So watch what he does. Not what he wrote, not what he swears—what he *does*, when there's nothing left in it for him."

She takes her coffee and goes to help Carlo with the computers, and leaves me alone in the main hall with the dying afternoon light and the wreckage of a celebration that never came.

My phone buzzes one more time, face-down on the sill. I turn it over.

DECLAN:

I'm not giving up on Highland. I'm not giving up on us. Please don't give up either.

I read it twice. Then I delete it, the way I'll delete the next one, and the one after that, until he understands that some bridges don't get rebuilt with words.

Tomorrow I'll start the legal challenges. Tomorrow I'll go looking for the thing that puts Highland beyond the reach of any boardroom—the thing my father might have found if he'd had more time, and I might have found if I'd had more sense than to trust the man holding the wrecking ball. Tomorrow I'll learn to fight Pierce Enterprises without Declan Pierce as an ally, because the truth is I never really had him as one.

Tonight, I just want to sit in my father's community center and remember what it feels like to be home—before home disappears, and before I let myself believe, even for one more moment, that anyone in a glass tower was ever going to save it for me.

16

Declan

THE PARKING STRUCTURE is the quietest place I've stood in years.

Maya's taillights vanish up the ramp, and I'm left three levels underground holding the folder she pressed into my chest, in a silence so complete I can hear an engine ticking as it cools somewhere down the row of cars.

Every instinct I've spent thirty-two years sharpening tells me to go after her—to close the distance and find the angle that wins, because that is what my father built me to do, and there has always, always been an angle.

But there isn't one here.

I look down at the folder instead. Harrison's work; I'd know his timing anywhere, the surgical generosity of a man who hands you a blade and calls it transparency. He watched me fight for Highland and lose, and then he decided the surest way to keep me on a leash was to make certain the one person whose opinion had come to matter to me would never trust me again.

The worst part, standing here in the dark, is that it worked—and it worked because every word on the page is mine.

I open the folder, though I don't need to. *I want us to control the narrative. Alternatives we'll help her discover don't exist.* I read the lines the way Maya must have read them an hour ago, for the first time, while her whole body still believed we'd lost something together—and I understand, at last and completely, that there is no version of this in which I get to be the man who meant the back half without also being the man who wrote the front.

I don't call her. She was clear, and she's earned the right to her silence, and chasing her down the way I'd chase a stalled negotiation would only prove I still believe every problem bends to enough pressure.

But somewhere on the drive home, stopped at a red light I don't remember reaching, I start to write anyway.

Maya, please. Let me explain.

The light turns green. I send it before I can talk myself out of it, the way I'll send the next one, and the one after that, into a silence that gives nothing back.

I know how the folder reads. I know what it looks like. Give me ten minutes.

Nothing. Of course, nothing. She told me in the garage exactly what I'd done—turned every good memory into a question—and a person doesn't answer the one who taught her to doubt the asking.

I set the folder on the passenger seat, and I drive home to a house that has never felt emptier, with no idea yet how long the silence I've earned is going to last.

. . .

The conference room feels different at 9 AM on a Monday morning, though I can't quite put my finger on why. I'm sitting at the same mahogany table where Highland's fate was decided two weeks ago, listening to Harrison outline the Anderson Project's accelerated timeline with the kind of satisfaction that comes from watching carefully laid plans unfold on schedule.

"Site preparation begins in three weeks," Harrison announces. "Highland Community Center has been cooperative with the relocation process, which should minimize community opposition during demolition."

Highland has been cooperative. The phrase makes my jaw clench. Maya has spent two weeks coordinating Highland's evacuation with the efficiency of someone who's accepted defeat, who's channeled her considerable organizational skills into adaptation rather than resistance. From Pierce Enterprises' perspective, her leadership during the transition makes our demolition timeline much smoother.

From my perspective, watching Maya manage Highland's dissolution while refusing to speak to me has been excruciating.

"Any concerns about community backlash during demolition?" Patricia asks, though her question sounds perfunctory rather than genuinely concerned.

"Highland's director has been very professional about the transition," Harrison replies, and I catch the pointed way he emphasizes "professional." "No protests, no media campaigns, no legal challenges. The community appears to have accepted the board's decision."

Because Maya chose survival over symbolic resistance. Because she's proven she can lead Highland through its worst crisis without anyone's help, including mine. Because she's evolved beyond needing rescue from corporate CEOs who make promises they can't keep.

"Declan?" Harrison's voice cuts through my internal processing. "You've been quiet this morning. Any observations about the transition process?"

Five pairs of eyes focus on me, and I realize this is another test. Harrison has been conducting these subtle evaluations for two weeks, probing whether my judgment remains compromised by personal feelings, whether I can represent Pierce Enterprises' interests despite my advocacy for Highland's preservation.

"The transition has proceeded more smoothly than anticipated," I say carefully. "Highland's leadership demonstrated exceptional organization and community coordination during a difficult process."

"Highland's leadership." Donovan Rice leans forward slightly. "You mean Miss Navarro specifically?"

Another probe. Another opportunity to prove my professional objectivity by discussing Maya like she's a business problem rather than the woman I fell for while learning traditional dances in her community center.

"Miss Navarro's management of Highland's relocation has been impressive from a logistical standpoint," I reply. "Coordinating program transitions across multiple partner organizations while maintaining service continuity requires significant organizational skills."

It's true, professional, and completely inadequate for describing what I've witnessed over the past two weeks. Maya has accomplished something extraordinary—leading Highland's community through devastating loss while preserving everything that actually matters about their gathering place. She's proven that Highland's value was never about the building Pierce Enterprises is demolishing.

She's also proven she doesn't need me to save what she cares about most.

"Good," Harrison says with approval that feels like condescension. "I'm glad to see you're maintaining appropriate perspective on the situation."

Appropriate perspective. As if my "inappropriate perspective" was the problem rather than Pierce Enterprises' inability to recognize Highland's value before voting for its destruction.

"Now, regarding the Westside project," Harrison continues, opening another folder. "Given the Anderson Project's success, the board is considering expanding our approach to similar community-adjacent developments. Declan, I'd like your assessment of acquisition opportunities in areas with comparable community resistance patterns."

I stare at Harrison, processing what he's asking. Pierce Enterprises wants to replicate the Highland model—identify community centers and gathering places, acquire the properties, demolish existing facilities, and build luxury developments that serve entirely different populations. They want me to use everything I learned from Highland's destruction to target other communities for the same fate.

"I'm not sure I understand the question," I say slowly.

"Community organizations often occupy valuable real estate at below-market rates," Melanie explains. "Highland demonstrated that these groups can be encouraged to relocate voluntarily if the process is managed professionally. We'd like to identify similar opportunities."

"You want me to find other community centers to demolish."

"We want you to identify underutilized properties with development potential," Harrison corrects. "Properties where community organizations might benefit from relocation assistance and partnership opportunities."

The euphemisms are careful, corporate, designed to make systematic community displacement sound like business strategy. But the underlying message is clear—Highland was a template, not an exception. Pierce Enterprises wants to scale this approach across Los Angeles.

"What kind of timeline are we discussing?" I ask, though every instinct tells me to refuse immediately.

"Preliminary market analysis within sixty days. Property acquisition strategy within six months." Harrison makes notes on his tablet. "This could position Pierce Enterprises as the premier developer for transit-adjacent community sites."

Transit-adjacent community sites. Another euphemism for the gathering places that anchor neighborhoods, that provide services for families who can't afford alternatives, that preserve cultural traditions and support networks for communities Pierce Enterprises has never bothered to understand.

"I'll need time to consider the scope and methodology," I tell Harrison.

"Of course. But Declan, I want to emphasize the importance of this project for your continued leadership development within the company." Harrison's smile doesn't reach his eyes. "Successfully implementing community-responsive acquisition strategies could establish you as an industry innovator."

The threat is subtle but unmistakable. My future at Pierce Enterprises depends on proving I can replicate Highland's destruction on a larger scale. That I've learned the right lessons from Maya's heartbreak and Highland's dissolution.

That I can be trusted to prioritize profit over the principles that made me question Pierce Enterprises' approach in the first place.

After the meeting ends, I retreat to my office and close the door, needing space to process what just happened. Harrison wants me to become the architect of systematic community displacement. To use my relationship with Maya, my understanding of Highland's value, my insight into community dynamics to identify targets for corporate acquisition.

It's the logical evolution of Pierce Enterprises' business model. It's also a betrayal of everything Maya taught me about what makes developments valuable beyond their profit margins.

My phone sits on my desk, Maya's contact information just a few touches away. For two weeks, I've been drafting and deleting messages, trying to find words that might bridge the gulf between Highland's destruction and the feelings that developed between us. Every attempt sounds like excuse-making or damage control.

But this morning's meeting changes the stakes. Harrison isn't just asking me to accept Highland's demolition—he's asking me to ensure that Highland becomes the first casualty in a much larger campaign.

My computer chimes with an email from Harrison:

Declan, attached are preliminary market analyses for three potential community acquisition targets. Please review and provide initial assessment by Friday. Looking forward to your insights on replicating the Highland model.

Three communities. Three potential Highlands, with their own Maya Navarros fighting to preserve what matters most to families who depend on community gathering places.

I delete the email without opening the attachments.

There's a knock on my office door—not Jessica's polite announcement, but the confident rap of someone who doesn't wait for permission. The door opens and Elliot walks in, carrying two cups of coffee and wearing an expression I recognize from fifteen years of friendship—he's about to deliver uncomfortable truths I need to hear.

"You look like hell," he says, settling into his usual chair and sliding one coffee across my desk.

"I feel worse than I look." I accept the coffee gratefully, noting how Elliot has made it exactly the way I've preferred since college—strong enough to fuel crisis management, no cream to dilute the impact. "What brings you to my fortress of professional isolation?"

"Concern for my best friend, who's been sitting in this office for two weeks looking like someone stole his dog." Elliot settles back in his chair, studying my expression with the kind of attention that comes from years of reading my moods. "Plus, I heard about this morning's board meeting. Harrison wants you to systematize Highland's destruction?"

"He wants me to identify 'underutilized properties with development potential.' Three communities to start, expansion plan to follow." I run my hand through my hair, feeling the weight of impossible choices. "Apparently Highland was such a successful template that Pierce Enterprises wants to scale the approach."

"And you told him?"

"I told him I'd consider the scope and methodology." The words sound pathetic even to me. "Which is corporate speak for 'I need time to figure out how to refuse without destroying my career entirely.'"

Elliot is quiet for a moment, his gaze drifting toward my windows that overlook the arts district. From here, Highland Community Center is invisible among the maze of buildings, but its presence hangs between us like unfinished business.

"Dec, can I ask you something? And I need you to answer honestly."

"Of course."

"Do you actually want to save your career at Pierce Enterprises, or do you want to save your reputation in an industry that's fundamentally opposed to what you've learned matters?"

The question cuts straight to the heart of everything I've been avoiding. For two weeks, I've been trying to figure out how to honor what Maya taught me about building things that matter while maintaining my position within Pierce Enterprises' corporate structure. But maybe the real problem isn't finding ways to change Pierce Enterprises— maybe it's accepting that the company my father built and my principles are fundamentally incompatible.

"I want to build something meaningful," I tell Elliot. "I

want to prove that business success and community preservation can coexist. I want to create developments that strengthen neighborhoods instead of displacing them."

"Then why are you trying to do that from within a company that just asked you to systematize community displacement?"

Because it's the only professional identity I've ever known. Because walking away from Pierce Enterprises means walking away from my father's legacy. Because starting over at thirty-two feels terrifying when I've spent my entire adult life building expertise in a specific approach to development.

"Because I don't know how to build something meaningful outside Pierce Enterprises' structure," I admit.

Elliot leans forward, his expression growing more animated. "What if you didn't need this structure? What if you had enough capital to operate independently?"

"Elliot, I have the money, but I don't have the infrastructure. Projects like Highland require development teams, legal frameworks, regulatory relationships that take years to build—"

"Dec, you're overthinking this," Elliot interrupts. "Highland isn't a massive development project—it's a single property purchase. About fifteen to twenty million. And here's what you don't know—Maya's been working on this problem too."

I set down my coffee cup. "What do you mean?"

"You know why Maya isn't answering your calls? She's not wallowing or giving up. She hired a specialized community development law firm to research community land trusts. She's been at City Hall every day for two weeks getting preliminary approvals. She's coordinated community input sessions and drafted legal frameworks."

The words hit me like cold water. "She's been doing all this alone?"

"She's been preparing to save Highland herself. The only thing she can't do is come up with the money to actually buy the property, at least not in time to stop the demolition. But she's built the entire legal structure. All the paperwork is ready to go."

I stare at Elliot, processing what he's telling me. While I've been wallowing in corporate guilt and trying to find words to apologize, Maya has been working toward the same solution I never thought to consider.

"How do you know all this?"

"My contact at the planning commission mentioned seeing Highland Community Center filings for community land trust establishment. So I did some digging." Elliot pulls out his phone. "Maya spent her father's life insurance money—about two hundred thousand—to hire Kemp & Associates, the firm that specializes in community land trusts. She's been preparing to save Highland through community ownership."

"Her father's life insurance money." The magnitude of what Maya has sacrificed hits me. "She spent her inheritance trying to save Highland."

"She spent it preparing the legal framework that *could* save Highland, *if* someone could provide the capital." Elliot leans forward. "She couldn't afford to hire just anyone—Kemp & Associates charges premium rates because they're the best at navigating these complex legal structures. But their work means everything is ready to go."

The idea is elegant, radical, and suddenly possible. Maya has already done the hardest part—navigating the legal complexities, getting community input, securing preliminary approvals. I could provide the capital that would activate her months of preparation.

"You're suggesting I buy Highland from Pierce Enterprises using Maya's legal framework?"

"I'm suggesting you honor the work she's already done while proving that some things are worth more than corporate loyalty." Elliot's voice grows more passionate. "She built the road, you provide the car. It's not rescue—it's partnership."

I walk to my office windows, looking out toward the arts district where Highland Community Center sits, scheduled for demolition in three wees. The building is still intact, still structurally sound, still perfectly suited for community programming. And somewhere in the city, Maya has been working tirelessly to create a legal structure that could save it permanently.

"What about Maya's reaction? She's spent two weeks thinking Highland was lost forever while secretly preparing to save it herself. How do I tell her I could have provided the missing piece all along?"

"You tell her you learned something from watching her refuse to give up. That you realized preserving communities shouldn't depend on corporate generosity—it should be guaranteed through community ownership." Elliot joins me at the windows. "And you tell her you want to be her partner in creating something better than what Pierce Enterprises offers."

"And if she sees it as too little, too late?"

"Then you've still created a model for community land trusts that could protect other gathering places from suffering Highland's fate," Elliot says. "But Declan, Maya's been working toward the same solution you're considering. That's not coincidence—that's compatibility."

It's a compelling vision, but it's also terrifying in its implications. Buying Highland would mean breaking completely with Pierce Enterprises, with the business model my father built, with the only professional identity I've ever known.

It would also mean proving to Maya that some things—communities, principles... even love—are worth risking everything to protect.

"How quickly could something like this happen?" I ask.

"Property acquisition? One to two weeks if Pierce Enterprises is motivated to sell. Community land trust establishment? Maya's already done the groundwork. Highland could be back in community hands before demolition is scheduled to begin."

Before demolition begins. Before Highland's families lose their gathering place forever, I could restore it with guarantees that it would never be threatened again.

"Elliot, this is insane." I turn to face him, my heart pounding with something I haven't felt since before the board meeting—hope. Real, actionable hope instead of the helpless dread that's been eating at me for days.

"This is exactly what your grandfather would have done." Elliot's smile is knowing, affectionate. "Community investment, supporting local organizations, proving that business success can strengthen neighborhoods rather than displacing them. He'd be proud of you for considering it."

My grandfather, who believed a man's worth was

measured by what he contributed rather than what he accumulated. Who would have understood Highland's value the moment he walked through its doors. Who would have appreciated Maya's determination to save her community through legal innovation rather than corporate charity.

"And my father? What would Maxwell Pierce think about his son walking away from Pierce Enterprises to buy back a community center?"

"Your father built Pierce Enterprises to create lasting value," Elliot says carefully. "Maybe he'd understand that some kinds of value can't be measured in quarterly reports."

Maybe. But sitting in this office, reading Harrison's plans to systematize community displacement while learning that Maya has been working tirelessly toward the same solution I never considered, I realize I care less about my father's theoretical approval than about honoring Maya's extraordinary effort.

The person Maya fell for during Highland's heritage festival wouldn't help Harrison target three more communities for destruction.

That person would find another way.

"I need to make some phone calls," I tell Elliot.

"Financial advisor?"

"Legal team. If I'm going to buy Highland using Maya's community land trust framework, I want to coordinate with her legal work, not override it." I pick up my phone, scrolling through contacts. "This needs to be a true partnership from the beginning."

Elliot's grin is pure satisfaction. "Now you're thinking like your grandfather."

"I'm thinking like someone who learned what really

matters from a woman who never stopped fighting for community preservation, even when it seemed hopeless." I pause, considering the magnitude of what Maya has accomplished while I've been wallowing in corporate guilt. "Even if she never speaks to me again, Highland's community deserves to benefit from the legal framework she's created."

"She'll speak to you again," Elliot says confidently. "Especially when she realizes you're not just saving Highland—you're honoring months of work she thought was pointless."

Maybe. But I've drafted a dozen apologies in two weeks and deleted every one, because there's no sentence that unwrites what she read in that folder. So I'll stop looking for the words and do the thing instead.

I'm buying Highland because it belongs to her community and never should have been mine to sell—and because I want, just once, to do something right without first running the numbers on what it gets me.

If it brings Maya back, I'll be luckier than I deserve. If it doesn't, Highland still stands, her father's name still goes over the door, and Harrison loses.

I can live with that—even the half of it I'd give almost anything to avoid.

17

Maya

THE SMELL of coffee would permeate the air by now, Tita Sol unlocking the classrooms for morning ESL practice while asking me in her usual loud voice—she never did learn the art of an inside voice—about whether I'd eaten breakfast yet. Rosa would be arranging chairs in the main hall, humming old Filipino lullabies while Carlo tested the sound system and Mrs. Valdez claimed her favorite corner table for citizenship test review.

Instead, I stand alone in the empty main hall at 6 AM, watching the sunrise paint golden light across silent walls. In three hours, bulldozers will destroy not just this building, but every echo of the life that should be filling it right now—children's laughter, whispered prayers of new citizens, the rhythm of traditional dances that kept culture alive in a city that forgets its roots.

Today is demolition day. Today, my father's dream becomes dust.

My phone buzzes with a final email from Kemp &

Associates, the community development law firm I hired two weeks ago.

Maya, all community land trust documentation has been finalized and filed with the city. Preliminary approvals are in place. Unfortunately, without the capital to purchase the property, we cannot proceed to implementation. We're sorry we couldn't help save Highland in time.

Two hundred thousand dollars. My father's entire life insurance policy, spent on the best legal team in California for community land trust establishment. All of it useless without the fifteen to twenty million dollars needed to actually buy Highland from Pierce Enterprises.

I delete the email and slide my phone back into my pocket. The legal framework exists—sitting in some lawyer's filing cabinet like a blueprint for a house that will never be built. If I'd had more time, more money, if I'd discovered community land trusts six months ago instead of after Pierce Enterprises' board vote sealed Highland's fate.

If, if, if.

"Maya, anak, you shouldn't be here alone." Rosa's voice cuts through the morning silence. She's standing in Highland's doorway, her face etched with worry. Behind her, the parking lot is empty, surrounded by the chain-link fence Pierce Enterprises installed yesterday to keep people away from the demolition site.

"How did you get in?" I ask, though I'm grateful for her presence.

"Same way you did—through the gap behind the dumpster." Rosa steps inside, closing the door behind her. "I saw your car from the street and knew you'd found a way inside. I couldn't let you face this alone."

"I needed to be here when the bulldozers come. I needed to be the last person to say goodbye."

Rosa settles beside me on Highland's worn wooden floor. "He would be proud of how you've fought for this place, anak. Even if we couldn't save the building, you saved what matters most."

"Did I?" The question comes out raw, honest. "Highland is about to become rubble, and I couldn't stop it."

Through Highland's front windows, I can see the first news van pulling up across the street. Channel 7, probably here to document the demolition for a human-interest segment about community displacement in downtown LA.

"Have you heard anything from Declan?" Rosa asks quietly.

The question I've been dreading for three weeks. "He tried to call the first few days. I didn't answer." I pause, using the silence to rebuild emotional walls that threaten to crumble every time someone mentions his name. "Rosa, it doesn't matter what Declan is doing. Highland's programs are thriving in their new locations, the community is adapting beautifully, and we've proven that Highland's value was never about this building."

It's true, practical, and completely inadequate for describing the way my chest aches every time I drive past Pierce Enterprises' tower.

"Then trust me when I say that Alejandro would be proud of how you've led Highland through this crisis. But he would also want you to leave room in your heart for forgiveness."

"Forgiveness for what? For not being able to save Highland?" I say. "Maybe this is just the way things work. You win some. You lose some." *And sometimes you try everything but it's just not meant to be.*

"Maybe. Or maybe that young man is fighting battles you can't see from here."

Before I can tell Rosa she's wrong about Declan, my phone buzzes with an incoming call.

"Maya, where are you?" Lianne's voice carries an urgency that makes my pulse quicken.

"Highland. Saying goodbye before the demolition crew arrives. Why?"

"Because Channel 7 just reported that Pierce Enterprises' demolition has been indefinitely postponed. Something about 'new development complications' and 'alternative acquisition arrangements.' Maya, what if Declan found a way to save Highland?"

The possibility hits like cold water. For three weeks, I've been operating under the assumption that Highland's demolition was inevitable, that even my attempt at setting up the land trust was simply a case of too little, too late.

"Lianne, Pierce Enterprises doesn't change their minds about multimillion-dollar development projects based on last-minute guilt or romantic gestures."

"Maybe they do when their CEO makes them an offer they can't refuse. The kind where he buys Highland himself."

I stare at my phone, trying to process what Lianne just said. "How do you know that?"

"Because Tita Sol's niece works in Pierce Enterprises' accounting department, and she just texted that paperwork came through this morning for Highland's sale to something called the Navarro Community Trust." She pauses, then takes a deep breath before continuing, "Declan bought Highland. He actually bought it."

I stare at Rosa, unable to move, barely able to process what I'm hearing.

Declan bought Highland?

Not Pierce Enterprises, not some corporate entity looking for tax write-offs, but Declan Pierce personally purchased the building that was supposed to be demolished this morning?

"Maya?" Lianne's voice seems to come from very far away. "Are you there?"

"I'm here. I just—I need to understand what this means."

"It means Highland is safe. Permanently safe."

Highland is safe. The words should fill me with joy, relief, the kind of celebration that comes with winning impossible battles. Instead, I feel something closer to shock mixed with an emotion I can't name.

For three weeks, I've been building Highland's future around the assumption that this building was lost forever. I've created new partnerships, established alternative programs, proven that Highland's community could thrive anywhere.

And now Declan has unilaterally decided that Highland's building should be preserved after all.

"Maya, anak, what's wrong?" Rosa asks, noting my expression. "This is good news, yes? Highland is saved."

"Highland was already saved. The programs are running successfully in four different locations, the community is more connected than ever, and we've proven that Highland's value isn't dependent on this specific building." I'm pacing now, energy coursing through me that feels like anger mixed with something I don't want to examine too closely. "We didn't need rescuing."

"But if Highland can come home—"

"Highland is home wherever the community gathers. We learned that over the past three weeks." I stop pacing and stare at Rosa. "Rosa, what if I don't want Highland to be saved by Declan Pierce's checkbook? What if I want Highland to succeed because of community strength, not corporate charity?"

Rosa studies my expression with the kind of maternal insight that sees through defensive reactions to the hurt underneath. "What if Highland being saved isn't about you or Declan, but about giving the community choices they didn't have before?"

Before I can respond, the center's front door opens and Carlo walks in, carrying his laptop, his expression wild.

"Ate, did you hear about Highland?"

I nod. "I heard that Declan bought Highland. What I don't understand is why."

Carlo opens his laptop and pulls up what appears to be a news article. "It's all over the news. Look at this headline."

He turns the laptop toward me, and I find myself reading a LA Times article with the headline: "Tech Billionaire Saves Community Center from Demolition."

Tech billionaire. The phrase stops me cold. I scan the article, noting details about Declan's personal wealth from his early social media investments, his decision to purchase Highland independently from Pierce Enterprises, his resignation as CEO to pursue "community-focused development."

"Maya," Carlo says quietly, "there's something else. The

article says this isn't just about Highland. Declan Pierce left Pierce Enterprises completely. He's starting his own company focused on community preservation."

I stare at the laptop screen, trying to process what I'm reading. Declan hasn't just saved Highland—he's walked away from everything. His family's company, his father's legacy, the world that shaped him into who he thought he had to be.

It's a complete transformation from the corporate CEO I met a couple months ago.

"Where is he?" I ask Carlo.

"I don't know. The article just says Highland's ownership transfer is being finalized today."

"I need some air," I tell Rosa and Carlo, heading toward Highland's back exit.

Highland's small parking lot overlooks the arts district, with downtown LA's skyline visible in the distance. Pierce Enterprises' tower rises among the glass monuments to corporate power, but this morning it looks different. Less like a threat, more like a reminder that sometimes the most unexpected solutions come from the places you least expect them.

My phone rings with a call from Tito Ricky, who's probably been fielding legal questions since the news broke.

"Maya, I assume you've heard about Highland's change in ownership status?"

"I heard that Declan bought Highland," I say. "What I don't understand is how something like this happens overnight."

"It doesn't happen overnight." Tito Ricky's voice carries the quiet satisfaction of a man who's spent a lifetime inside complicated paperwork. "A community land trust takes weeks to assemble—property appraisal, financial documentation, community input, the city filings. None of that came together this morning, Maya. The legal groundwork has been in place for two weeks."

Two weeks. The same two weeks I spent at Kemp & Associates, spending the last of my father's life insurance on a framework I was certain would die in a filing cabinet for want of the millions I didn't have. The groundwork Tito Ricky means isn't two weeks of Declan quietly arranging Highland's rescue behind my back—it's mine. He couldn't have moved this fast on his own. He must have found the structure I'd already built and put his money behind it.

"Why didn't he tell me?"

"Maybe because he wanted to present you with a complete solution rather than another promise that might not materialize. Maybe because he learned something from watching you lead Highland through crisis without depending on anyone else's rescue efforts." Tito Ricky pauses. "The legal framework you created with Kemp & Associates—that's what made this possible. Declan didn't establish the land trust. He used your documentation and provided the capital to activate what you'd already built."

My heart is racing, the implications of my uncle's words beginning to overwhelm me. "What does this mean for Highland's programs? For the partnerships we've established over the past few weeks?"

"It means Highland has choices. The community can return to centralized programming in Highland's building, maintain the distributed model across multiple partner locations, or create some combination that serves families' evolving needs." There's a note of finality in Tito Ricky's voice as he adds, "Highland's future is entirely up to the community now."

Community choice. After weeks of adapting to circumstances beyond our control, Highland's families can decide for themselves what model works best for their needs.

"There's something else you should know," Tito Ricky continues. "The trust is named after your family. Declan Pierce specifically requested that Highland's protection honor your father's legacy and your leadership during the crisis."

The Navarro Community Trust. Highland's protection isn't just guaranteed through legal mechanisms—it's guaranteed through a foundation that bears my family's name, that recognizes my father's vision and my role in preserving it.

I sink onto the parking lot's concrete barrier, overwhelmed by the magnitude of what Declan has accomplished. He hasn't just saved Highland; he's created a permanent memorial to my father's work.

"Maya?" Tito Ricky's voice is gentle. "How are you feeling about all this?"

How am I feeling? Grateful, shocked, angry, hopeful, terrified, and completely in love with a man who just proved that some gestures are worth waiting for, even when you've given up hope they'll ever come.

"I'm feeling like I owe Declan Pierce a conversation," I admit.

"Good. Because I think he's been waiting for that conversation for a while now."

After Tito Ricky hangs up, I remain in Highland's parking lot, watching downtown LA wake up around me.

News vans are arriving, community members are gathering to witness Highland's salvation, and somewhere in the city, Declan Pierce is probably preparing to face the woman whose heart broke when they lost the fight together three weeks ago.

The woman he just gave every reason to believe in him again.

Rosa appears beside me with a fresh cup of coffee and the kind of knowing smile that means she's been watching my emotional processing from Highland's back windows.

"So." Rosa settles onto the concrete barrier beside me, close enough that her shoulder presses warm against mine. "Still think you had that young man figured out?"

"I told him in that parking garage that I'd never be able to trust which version of him was real." I take the coffee she's brought me, the way she's brought me coffee through every hard morning of my adult life. "I meant it, Rosa. I don't know how to unsay it."

"Who asked you to unsay it?" Her voice is gentle, unhurried. "A true thing stays true. You just have to set it next to what he did after you said it." She turns her cup slowly in her hands. "He didn't send you flowers, anak. He didn't send you a speech. He gave away his father's company and put your father's name on the one thing no one can ever knock down. A man doesn't do that to win an argument. He does it because he's decided who he wants to be."

I look out at the skyline, at the tower where six people once decided we weren't worth the trouble, and I let myself feel the thing I've been holding off for three weeks—the thing that's been there since some night between the storage room and the heritage festival, when Declan Pierce stopped being the man I came to fight.

I don't say it. Not out loud, and not even to Rosa, who has earned every other secret I own—because if those words are ever going to leave me, there's exactly one person who should hear them first, and he's across the city in a garden I've never seen, waiting to find out whether anything he did was enough.

Rosa watches my face the way she's watched it my whole life, and whatever she finds there makes her smile.

"You don't have to tell me," she says, patting my knee and pushing up off the barrier with a small grunt. "I've known since the Heritage Festival. Go tell the one who doesn't."

I sit a moment more with the cooling coffee and the sunrise and the building that's still standing when it shouldn't be. Then I get up to find my keys.

18
———

Declan

By now, three hours after the news broke, Maya knows.

I don't expect her to call. I glance at my phone anyway, silent on the garden table beside a tray of tomato seedlings I've been transplanting since the sun came up. It rang without stopping for the first hour—reporters, Pierce Enterprises executives demanding to know what I think I'm doing, a legal team assembling the last of the paperwork before this afternoon's press conference—until I set it face-down and went looking for something I could do with my hands that built instead of broke.

For three years I spent my mornings reviewing demolition schedules. This morning I'm pressing soil around a Cherokee Purple seedling in dirt my grandfather tended forty years ago, and it's the first work in longer than I can remember that I'm not ashamed of.

I don't expect her to thank me. In her place, I wouldn't thank a man for solving with a checkbook what he could have solved months earlier, and I wouldn't trust the timing of it either. That's the part I keep circling as I work—not whether she'll see the purchase as rescue, but whether she'll believe a single thing behind it, because the last time we stood face to face she was holding a folder full of my own words, and she told me I'd turned every good memory between us into a question.

You don't answer that with a press release. I tried, for three weeks, to find the sentence that would undo it, and there wasn't one—so I stopped writing sentences and started signing papers instead.

The doorbell pulls me out of it. I almost don't answer; the press conference is two hours off, and the garden is the first place I've been able to think since I resigned. But it rings again, and then I hear her voice through the gate, saying my name.

Maya.

I brush the soil from my hands onto jeans worn through at both knees and come around the side of the house to find her at my door in her Highland T-shirt, her hair pulled back, her expression doing the thing it does when she's decided something and hasn't yet said it out loud.

"Maya. I wasn't sure you'd come."

"Neither was I." She doesn't step closer. "I almost didn't."

For a moment I think she's come with conditions, a lawyer's list, an objection I'll have to answer. Instead she says, "I've read those board minutes maybe a hundred times in three weeks. I gave you the folder in the garage, but I didn't need to keep it. I know it by heart now." Her voice stays level, which is worse than if it shook. "The part where you stood in a room full of people and called the whole collaboration a way to keep me quiet and reasonable while you ran out the clock."

The folder she's talking about has been on my desk for three weeks, where I've kept it the way you keep a thing you're not allowed to look away from.

"And then I turned on the news this morning," she goes on, "and found out you'd resigned, and spent your own money to put Highland in a trust with my father's name on it. Declan, I came here because I need to understand which of those is the *real* you. Because I can't hold both."

There it is—the exact question I've been failing to answer for three weeks.

"They're both real," I say, and I watch her flinch, because it isn't the absolution she came for. "I wrote every word in that folder, and I meant it when I said it. I'm not going to stand in my grandfather's garden and pretend otherwise, because the last thing I did to you was lie, and I'm not starting there again."

She doesn't move.

"In the parking garage you told me I'd made it so you could never know which version was real, and you were right. I couldn't think of one thing to say that you'd have any reason to believe—every apology I drafted read like a man managing his own optics, which is exactly what I'd trained you to expect." I gesture, helplessly, at the house and the garden and the silent phone with its hundred missed calls. "So I stopped trying to say it. I resigned. I spent the money. I put your father's name on the one thing Harrison can never take back—not to win you, because I knew it might already be too late for that, but because it was the only answer I had that didn't depend on you believing my words. You can check every line of it. There's nothing in it for me."

Maya looks down at her empty hands, then back at me, and something in her shoulders lets go—not forgiveness, not yet, but the first loosening I've seen since she arrived.

"That's what I couldn't get past," she says quietly. "Every kind thing you ever said to me, I had to weigh against that folder, and I didn't have any way to tell the difference." She's quiet a moment. "But you can't fake walking away from your father's company. You can't fake my father's name on a trust you'll never make a dollar from." A breath. "This is the first thing you've done that I can't argue with."

"It doesn't erase it," she adds, and the edge comes back into her voice. "You could have bought Highland months ago. You could have spared all of it—the vote, the demolition notices, three weeks of moving programs into church basements while families wondered if they still had a home. You didn't think of it until Elliot told you I'd already done the work."

"You're right." I don't reach for an excuse. "For three years I solved everything through board votes and profit analyses. It never occurred to me that some things are too important to leave to corporate democracy—until I watched you refuse to leave Highland's survival in anyone's hands but the community's. You taught me that. I was just slow to learn it."

She wipes at her eyes with the back of her hand, and I make myself stay where I am instead of closing the distance.

"How much of my framework did you use?"

"All of it. Every document, every approval Kemp & Associates filed. Highland exists as a community land trust because you built the structure that made it legally possible —I only put up the capital that turned your blueprint into a building no one can vote away." I hold her gaze. "I named it the Navarro Community Trust because the work was yours and the vision was your father's. I'm just the one who showed up late with a checkbook."

"And it doesn't have to stop at Highland," I add. "What you built with Kemp & Associates is a template—other communities could use it to protect their gathering places before anyone ever hands them a demolition notice. If you want it to be, this is the beginning of something much larger than one building."

The tears she's been holding finally spill over.

"Come into the garden," I say. "I've been planting things instead of tearing them down. It's the only place that's made any sense in three weeks."

She follows me through the side gate, into the garden my grandfather built and my father ignored—past the raised beds and the staked tomatoes and the citrus hanging heavy on the branches—and she takes it in the way she takes in everything, completely, looking for what's real underneath.

"You did all this since you resigned?"

"The gardeners started it. I finished it." I crouch to check the soil around the Cherokee Purple. "Turns out I'd rather grow something than knock it down. Took me thirty-two years and one community organizer to work that out."

She's quiet for a long moment, and when she speaks the last of the armor has gone out of her voice. "Why did you really do it, Declan? The truth."

I stand, and I don't look away. "Because you showed me what it looks like to build something worth protecting.

Because I'd rather be your partner than Pierce Enterprises' CEO." A beat. "And because I love you—more than my father's company, more than his approval, more than anything I thought mattered before you walked into my lobby with eight hundred and forty-three signatures and told me exactly who I was."

"You didn't buy Highland to get me back." It isn't quite a question.

"No. I bought it because it was right, and because I wanted to be someone who'd have done it whether or not you ever spoke to me again." I close the space between us. "Wanting you back is the part I didn't let myself count on."

"I've been fighting this for three weeks," she says, and her hand comes up to rest against my chest, over the place where she once pressed that folder. "Angry was safer than admitting I never actually stopped." She doesn't finish the sentence. "I love you too. I think I have since you ate Rosa's siopao standing up in my kitchen and pretended you weren't terrified of every person in the room."

I laugh, surprised, and it loosens something in both of us.

"Then show me," she says. "Not the words. Show me what this looks like when we're finally on the same side."

I cup her face in hands that still smell of soil and growing things, and I kiss her—slow, and then not slow at all when she fists her fingers in my hair—and she tastes like coffee and the morning and every outcome I'd told myself I wasn't allowed to want.

When we break apart she keeps her forehead against mine. "Your hands smell like tomatoes."

"I've been at it since dawn."

She chuckles. "Don't apologize. It smells like something taking root."

Both our phones go off at once—hers in her bag, mine on the garden table beside the seedlings.

"The press conference," she says. "Highland's reopening."

"Highland's *homecoming*." I answer mine to Elliot's voice already mid-logistics; her screen shows Lianne's name. "Two hours," I tell her when I hang up. "Which is good, because I can't very well announce Highland's future with half my grandfather's flowerbed under my fingernails."

Maya

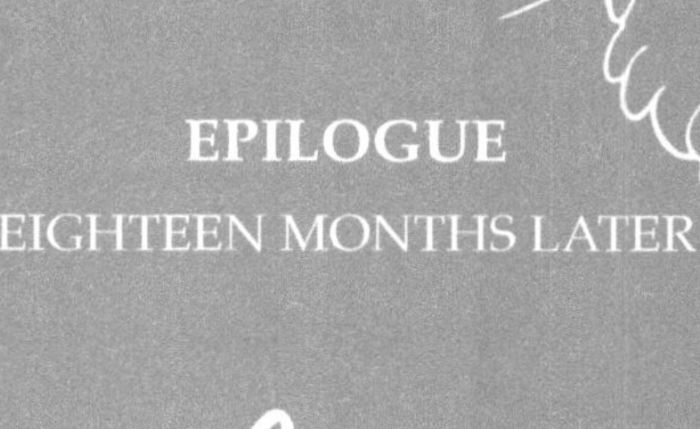

I STOP. I read my father's words—words I haven't seen written down in twenty years—and I can't get my breath around them.

"Declan." It comes out as almost nothing. "You named the assembly hall for my father."

"Highland's community named it for your father," he says. "I coordinated the plaque, and I made sure they used his words."

I trace the engraved letters with my fingertips. "How did you know that line? I never told you those exact words."

"Rosa did. She said Alejandro used it at every board meeting where someone told him Highland couldn't survive on the budget he had." His hand settles at the small of my back. "He didn't build this place with twenty-seven dollars, mahal. He built it on the idea that a community is worth more than what it costs."

I lean into him and let myself feel the whole distance we've come—from the woman who scattered petition signatures across his office floor to this, his hand warm against my spine in a hallway that carries my father's name. There was a stretch, after the board vote, when I was certain I'd never be able to believe a single thing this man told me, and I'd stood in a parking garage and said exactly that to his face. He didn't argue with me then. He just spent the next eighteen months proving me wrong without once asking me to take his word for it.

"Thank you," I whisper. "For Highland. For my father's name on that wall. For being someone I could come back to."

"Thank you for the petition," he says, and I feel him smile against my hair. "Everything good in my life started the morning you scattered eight hundred and forty-three signatures across my floor and told me exactly what kind of man I was."

I pull back to look at him. "I was so angry that day."

"You were magnificent that day." He brushes a tear off my cheek. "Furious and completely unafraid in a building designed to make people feel small. You rearranged my entire life in fifteen minutes and didn't even know it."

"We rearranged it," I tell him. "Together."

"Maya! Declan!" Carlo's voice carries down the hallway. "It's starting—everyone's asking for you two."

There's a title drifting around the celebration tonight—co-directors of the Navarro Community Foundation—that still makes me smile whenever I hear it. Eighteen months ago I was Highland's executive director, fighting to keep Declan's own company from putting it under a wrecking ball. Now I run Highland, he runs the foundation that protects the next Highland before it ever needs saving, and we are partners in every sense the word will hold.

The main hall is packed—three generations of families, a row of city officials, cameras at the back, and, beneath all of it, the people who turn Highland into Highland. Rosa works the food line. Tita Sol aims volunteers around the room like a traffic cop. Carlo drifts through the whole thing with his camera, missing nothing.

I step up onto the small stage and look out at twenty-one years of this place. The kids who learned to read in our library are raising kids of their own here now; in the front row, Lola Soledad sits beside a teenager born two miles from this building, the two of them splitting a plate of bibingka.

"Welcome to Highland's anniversary," I begin, and the room settles. "Tonight we're not only celebrating that Highland survived. We're celebrating what it became after it almost didn't."

I find Rosa's face in the crowd, and Tito Ricky's, and a hundred others I've known for half my life. "Two years ago, a company decided this building was worth more as luxury condos than as the place it already was. They were wrong, and you proved it—not with money, because we never had any, but by showing up. Eight hundred and forty-three of you put your names to that."

"Highland belongs to its community now, in writing, in a way no board vote and no developer can ever undo. We own our home, and we get to decide what it's for—for as long as there are Navarros and Reyeses and Santoses willing to fight for it."

The applause goes long, and when it finally fades I realize Declan is crossing toward the stage. He climbs the steps with that easy confidence of his, all of it except his hands, which won't quite hold still.

"Thank you, Maya." He turns to the room. "When I first walked through these doors, I thought Highland was a problem to be solved. I'd built an entire career on the belief that a place like this and a business like mine could never both win." A few knowing laughs. "Maya and this community spent six weeks proving me wrong, and the two years since proving it again every single day."

The room has gone quiet in the way rooms do when they feel something coming. Declan's voice drops into the register I used to hear only late at night, when he talked about his mother, or his father, or the man he was afraid he'd never stop being.

"This place taught me that the things actually worth protecting are the ones you can't put a price on." He steps closer, his eyes only on me now. "And it taught me what it's like to build something beside a person who makes you better at the building."

"Eighteen months ago, I thought I'd invested in a community center." He draws a small box from his jacket.

"What I'd really found was the one person I want next to me for whatever I build for the rest of my life."

My heart is going too fast to hear over. Around the room everyone has gone still—Rosa with both hands pressed to her mouth, Tita Sol gripping the back of a chair, Carlo with his camera already up—and I understand all at once that every person I love has been keeping this from me for weeks.

He goes down on one knee on Highland's floor, and the ring catches the light from the new chandeliers.

"Maya Navarro. You walked into my office two years ago with eight hundred and forty-three signatures, scattered half of them across my carpet, and you have been turning my life into something worth living ever since." His voice doesn't shake, but his hands do. "Marry me. Build the rest of it with me."

The silence stretches, and two years move through me in a single breath—the day I was certain I'd lost Highland for good, and the morning I learned he'd walked away from everything he had in order to give it back.

"Yes," I say, and Highland's new acoustics carry it to every corner of the room. "Yes. Of course, yes."

The hall comes apart in cheering. Declan slides the ring onto my finger—a vintage piece, old and a little imperfect and lovelier for it—and then he's kissing me while every person I love makes an unreasonable amount of noise around us.

"I love you," I tell him against his mouth.

"I should hope so," he murmurs. "I gave up a Fortune 500 company on the strength of it." Then, with none of the joke left in his voice: "I love you, Maya. You're the only thing I ever wanted badly enough to become someone new to deserve."

For a while there's nothing but congratulations and the ring passing hand to hand and Rosa already arguing with Tita Sol over whether the wedding lumpia should be Shanghai-style. Carlo photographs all of it, the way he photographs everything, so that tonight becomes one more thing Highland gets to keep.

"How long have you been planning this?" I ask Declan when we finally find a pocket of quiet.

"Weeks. Rosa timed the plaque so it would be ready tonight. Tita Sol made sure half the neighborhood would be in the room." He tips his head toward Carlo. "And he's been threatening to hang the photos on every wall in the building."

"Newsletter first," Carlo calls, not bothering to pretend he wasn't listening.

The band slides into something slow, and Declan finds me before I can vanish back into the logistics of my own party, his hand closing warm around mine and drawing me onto the floor whether I've agreed to it or not. Two years ago this man couldn't have found the rhythm of a Tinikling with both hands and a map; tonight he gathers me in close, one palm spread low against my spine, and moves like he's spent his whole life learning the particular way I like to be held. I tuck my face into the warm hollow beneath his jaw and breathe him in, and I feel rather than hear the low sound he makes when my mouth grazes his throat.

"You keep doing that," he murmurs into my hair, his hand pressing me closer, "and I'm going to forget there are three hundred people watching."

"Let them watch." But the heat climbs my neck anyway, and I can feel the answering tension in him, eighteen months that have done nothing at all to dull the way my body still answers his. "Besides," I add, lifting my face until the words land against his lips, "the celebration ends eventually. And then it's just us, and that garden of yours, and a very long night with no one needing either of us to coordinate a single thing."

His breath catches—I've learned exactly how to make it catch—and his eyes go dark in a way that has nothing to do with community land trusts. "Maya Navarro," he says, low and rough, "you are going to be the death of every plan I have ever made."

"I certainly hope so." And I kiss the corner of his mouth and let him turn me back into the music.

When the song ends, someone steals Declan away to talk foundation business, and for a few minutes no one needs anything from me. I drift to the edge of the floor and look at the room my father raised on twenty-seven dollars, and the wing that finally carries his name, and the man across the floor who turned out to be nothing like the one I marched in to fight.

I spent most of my life believing people could change. For about three weeks—after a board vote and a folder full of his own cold words—I was terrified I'd been wrong, that his change had been the most convincing lie I'd ever let myself fall for. Tonight, with his ring on my hand and my father's name on the wall, I finally have my answer.

Some things are worth the risk.

My father knew it with twenty-seven dollars and a paintbrush.

I learned it with eight hundred and forty-three signatures, a man I was sure was my enemy, and the slow, stubborn proof that he never really was.

And what he is now, I get to call mahal for the rest of my life—my love, and my home.

~

*Thank you so much for reading **Worth the Risk**. I hope you enjoyed Maya and Declan's story!*

*Elliot's book is **Worth the Fight: A Reverse Age Gap Romance***

*Lianne's book is **Worth the Wait: A Second Chance CEO Romance***

She had the plan. He had forever.

Cassie's life is mapped out: six months as COO, then back to San Francisco for solo motherhood. No dependencies. No trust.

Until her CEO turns out to be Elliot Walker—her former student who never got over her.

Working together means chemistry they can't ignore. But a hostile board is watching, and her fertility appointment is weeks away.

When everything explodes, someone has to sacrifice. Someone has to be brave enough to fight.

Will she choose the safe plan—or the man who's been waiting eight years?

Second chance CEO romance. Age gap. Forbidden love.

HE CHOSE HIS FAMILY OVER HER HEART.

NOW HE WANTS A SECOND CHANCE.

Four years ago, billionaire Cameron Judd broke event planner Lianne Peralta's heart when family pressure forced him to end their relationship.

Now she's planning his company's anniversary gala.

Lianne built her success without him—and she's not about to let him back into her life, no matter how much he's changed or how sorry he claims to be.

But Cameron's not giving up. He lost her once to cowardice, and he'll do whatever it takes to prove he's finally ready to choose love over everything else.

Even if it means risking everything he has left.

Sometimes the biggest risk is loving someone who already broke your heart.

OTHER BOOKS BY LIZ DURANO

A DIFFERENT KIND OF LOVE: TAOS

Everything She Ever Wanted

Breaking the Rules

Where She Belongs

Home to You

Other Side of Love

Everything that Remains

A DIFFERENT KIND OF LOVE: NEW YORK

Falling for Jordan

Friends with Benefits

More than Pretend

WORTH IT ALL

Worth the Fight

Worth the Wait

LOVE BEACH EVER AFTER

Summer with a Navy SEAL

Merry with a Tycoon

Spring Break with a Bodyguard

<u>**MULTI-AUTHOR SERIES**</u>

Wrong Cabin Right Mountain Man

All of You: Heart of a Wounded Hero

Working for Keeps

<u>**ROMANCE ANTHOLOGIES**</u>

Forevermore

Love at the Fiesta

<u>**LOVE AT THE SORAYA**</u>

The Replacement Fiance

The Reluctant Fiancee

<u>**CELEBRITY SERIES**</u>

Loving Ashe

Loving Riley

ABOUT THE AUTHOR

Although Liz studied Journalism in college, she discovered that she preferred writing fiction over ad copy, and so these days, she writes women's fiction and romance.

She lives in Southern California with her family and Truffles, a senior Chihuahua mix who keeps guard of her writing space and a growing pile of books (and wool for when she needs to spin for inspiration).

You can follow Liz's book adventures by visiting lizdurano.com

facebook.com/lizduranobooks

instagram.com/lizdurano

bookbub.com/authors/liz-durano